The Hermit of the Brule River

An Alphonse "Dave" Davecki Novel

Previous Davecki Novels

Death by Corvette

Something in the Water

Burn Baby Burn

Lake Effect

Lord of the Rinks

Death on the Brule River

Gold Greed and Good Dogs

This Davecki novel is a "true" Paige Turner!

The Hermit of the Brule River

Michael Savage

Mike Savage

Bois Brule Publications

First Edition – First Printing

Reader Alert: In this and other Davecki books
Sauna
is a verb.

ISBN-13: 978-1-937706-26-5
Library of Congress Control Number: 2022930574

Front Cover Art: Amy Eliot
Back Cover Art: Sarah Keefer

Published by:

Bois Brule Publications, with Winneboujou Valley Press, with Burnt River Press, and also with you, Hackmatack Publications, all fake gnus imprints of

Savage Press
14172E Carlson Rd.
Brule, WI 54880

with branch, twig, and, leaf orifices in New Yorkie, Lendon Englond , Kidney Australis, San Francesspool, Pour-us France, Fatcow Russia, Burrrlin Churmany, Pokeyman Japan, and Pillvaawki, Viscawnsun.

Phone: 218-391-3070
Email: mail@savpress.com
Website: www.savpress.com

Printed in the United States of America

"A hermit is simply a person to whom civilization has failed to adjust itself."

– Will Cuppy

Prologue

The Copper Canyon
Batopilas, Chihuahua, Mexico

"Mama?"

"Yes, hijo?"

"Why is my skin so white and you and papa so brown?"

Maria Lopez paused her cooking. She looked at her son and said, "Can you lift the bucket full of water from the well?"

The boy gazed at his mama for a moment, answered, "No."

Mama resumed preparing the meal, studying her tortilla flour as she spoke. "Right now the answer to your question is like the full water bucket, too heavy for you to lift. When you are older and stronger, strong enough to lift heavy burdens, we will answer your question. For now, go out and play, grow strong, soon enough you will carry your burdens well."

Jason Lopez studied his mother's downcast face, blinked his blue eyes and said, "Yes, mama."

1

The mellow sunlight of the setting spring sun slathered the top of the 150-foot tall white pine growing at the edge of the Bois Brule river butter yellow. A large black crow sat on the pine's terminal leader like a black flag waving gently in the wind. "Caw-caw-caw," the crow called as a vintage cream-colored Ford Bronco left the driveway of the cabin situated thirty yards back across the mowed lawn sliding down to river's edge. At Grandfather Pine's forty-inch thick base a man in tattered black clothing rose from his repose in the niche of the mighty tree's massive root shoulders. Moving quietly and with sure intent through a patch of woodsy brush, the man stepped from the forest's concealment to the edge of the one-acre lawn.

The black bearded man raised his face to the sky and said, "Caw-caw-caw," in a horrible attempt at corvus talk. Reverting to English, he said, "Thank's Elvis." He looked down at the masked face of the portly raccoon at his feet. "Come on El." He hustled across the green grass, the fat raccoon humping at his heels.

At the log home he tried the rear door. Locked. "Odd," he muttered.

He looked at the firewood pile stacked against the log wall under the two-foot overhanging eave. Above the pile, a double-hung vinyl window installed horizontally. The stack was neat and sturdy looking. He scratched the back of his head, looked at the blue cloudless sky with the black form of Elvis circling a hundred feet above. Looking at the woodpile again and studying the window, the man in black commenced to climbing.

As he ascended, chunks of wood fell to the ground. Eleanor clawed her way to the top, also dislodging wood chunks as she went. They looked like spiders climbing, one itsy-bitsy and furry, the other a mutated arachnid in a '50s sci-fi movie.

At the white-sashed window with lace curtains inside, the climber's deft and dirty fingers pulled a butter knife from the

Captain Kangaroo pocket of his rather well-abused Stormy Kromer wool Mackinaw. He pried the thin aluminum channel of the window frame back, kinking the channel permanently. He inserted his calloused finger in the gap and pulled until the screen popped out. He set the now crooked screen aside.

"Sorry, folks," he mumbled. His black moustache and beard moved, the only visible indication of speech.

"Chitter-chit," Eleanor said.

"I know, El. I feel bad too," the man said.

He wiggled the knife between the window sashes and worked it until the sash-lock moved aside. He pushed the window open. On the sill, a multi-color Oulu Glass dish. The burglar moved the swirl plate to the counter below and leaned in. Like a dog digging into a gopher hole, he climbed head first into a roomy kitchen, the rump of his black wool pants looking like a black bear's hairy behind.

Eleanor clambered in after.

The burglar slid the window shut. He relocked it. He shuffled to the refrigerator. He opened the door, took out a plastic gallon jug of milk, removed the blue cap, and swigged a long pull. Dots of milk looking like white aphid larvae on the underside of a rotting piece of blackened tamarack bark stuck to the dark black hairs of his long bushy beard. The white dots complimented the faint waves of dull gray streaking the beard like high cirrus clouds on a summer day.

"Ahhh," he exhaled. He went to the dishwasher with a DIRTY sign magnetized to the stainless steel fascia. He opened the door, pulled out a dish, set it on the floor, and poured milk.

Eleanor lapped like a thirsty cat.

The man took another pull from the jug, capped it and returned it to the fridge. He stroked his whiskers, erasing the milky bugs with two swipes.

He went to the line of drawers under the gray granite countertop between the sink and the door to the living room. Opening drawers one by one, he stopped at the last drawer next to the door. He lifted a half-full, or empty, 24-pack of AA batteries from the drawer. He stuffed the batteries into the pocket with the knife. Above the counter he opened successive cupboard doors until the canned goods appeared. Green beans, corn, peas, and peach slices in light syrup stood in orderly ranks like tin soldiers at attention. He volunteered eight different soldiers, leaving the rest. He put the cans on the counter. He returned to the fridge and pulled a green *Keep It Clean* environmentally friendly tote bag from between the fridge and the log wall. He put the cans unfriendly to the environment in the bag. He opened the last door above the counter. "Umm," he said, pulling down a partially open plastic tray of Oreo cookies half-full or empty. He put the treats in the bag and carried it to the living room.

Eleanor finished her milk and followed.

The man went to the bookcase beside the stone fireplace and set the bag down.

The raccoon shuttled to the bag, rose up on heavy haunches and pulled a cookie free.

"You're supposed to be on a diet, El," the man said.

The raccoon flicked a beady-eyed glance at her accuser and pulled back black lips showing white teeth in a grin or a snarl. "Chitt-chitt."

"Whatever," the man replied. He ran his finger along the book backs on the middle shelf. A stuffed pine marten on top of the seven-foot-tall shelf held an eternal pose bent down over the oak trimmed edge, seeming to observe the dirt-encrusted fingernail running along each spine. At *Under the Dome,* the finger pulled. He tried to put the thick book in his remaining empty coat pocket, failed, and put it in the bag.

He went to the fireplace. He picked up the unholstered revolver setting on the spaulted maple mantel. He brought the muzzle close to his nose and sniffed. "Hmm." He put the gun back. At the end of the mantel he twisted the framed black-and-white 8x10 autographed photo of Dwight D. Eisenhower more toward the room and pushed it back a little, aligning it with the companion photo of Calvin Coolidge.

He walked to the round maple table beside a leather-covered La-Z-Boy recliner and plopped the green booty sack to the wide plank flooring with a clunk. He lifted a book with a protruding bookmark off the round side table and gazed long at the cover, transfixed by the Navajo art. He opened the pages to the bookmark and read a few lines. He made a motion to put the book in the bag but stopped. He looked at the cover again. He shrugged and tossed the book to the seat of the recliner. The book pages fluttered. The bookmark fell out.

He went to the dining room table at the opposite end of the open room. A half-finished puzzle covered the table top. Putting down his bag, he picked up the top of the thousand-piece puzzle box. He studied the image of white-capped mountains and blue stream flowing past yellow-leaved aspen and the little log cabin with white smoke coming from the chimney. He put the lid down. Studying the jumbled puzzle, he picked up the open topped box of Cheez-Its from the edge of the table without looking. He dumped a tumble of crackers onto his palm while studying the puzzle. He stuffed the orange crackers into his whisker enshrouded maw. He chewed. Orange flakes fell to his beard and the table. Chewing like a Holstein working its cud, his piercing deep blue eyes scanned the pieces.

From the floor, Eleanor chittered. The burglar tossed another cracker in her direction. She caught it mid-air and flopped onto her back, holding the prize in her front paws like it was manna from heaven then nibbling on the delicacy while a "girrring" sound hummed out of her throat.

The Burglar chose a single puzzle piece from the tabletop. The puzzle piece had a tendril of white smoke against a blue background. He snapped it into place above the chimney, completing the snake of smoke rising from the picture perfect cabin.

Eleanor squirmed on her back, swallowed the last of her Cheez-It and growled. She raised her front paws like she was slain in the spirit at a Pentecostal prayer meeting.

Hermit tossed her another cracker and stuffed the box in with the cookies and canned goods.

Eleanor enjoyed her ecstasy.

The burglar went to the oak six-panel door at the far side of the room, opened it and stepped to the wide porch outside. He held the door open, "Vaminose, El."

Eleanor crunched the cracker down, rolled to her side, made two attempts to gain her feet, and, finally succeeding, scuttled across the floor.

"I have one word for you, El," Hermit said, "Diet with a capital D."

Eleanor shot him a look of death, scooted through the door to the porch and down the steps to the lawn.

"It's not my fault you're overweight," the burglar said. He went to the end of the open porch. He freed the propane tank from the oversized chrome Weber gas grill backed against the cedar branch balusters of the hand-crafted railing. He hefted the tank. "Half full," he said. He returned to his booty bag and laid his propane burden down. He returned to the front door and straightened the crooked BALLY O'GRADY planchette nailed to the log wall beside the entrance. He went inside, returned to the recliner and grabbed the book, stuffing it in the other Captain Kangaroo pocket. On the way out he picked the black and red Stormy Kromer hat off the coat hook next to the entry. He tried the hat on. It smooshed his tangle of black hair down as he pulled it tight. "Fits."

At that moment Elvis swooped past the porch in a black streak. "Caw-caw-caw," he scratched out.

"Okay! Thanks!" the burglar acknowledged. Slamming the door, he grabbed his merchandise, and sprinted across the green grass lawn toward the river's edge. As he melted into the forest, the cream colored classic Bronco nosed out of the woods into the driveway.

Huffing from the sprint the burglar dropped the white tank and leaned the green bag against Grandfather Pine's huge trunk. He put his palms on his thighs and panted. Eleanor scampered to the green bag and pulled it over. Oreos spilled out.

"Chica mala. Bad girl," the man said between huffs. Calmer now, he walked to a wind-fall, moss-covered balsam tree rotting into the ground.

Eleanor ignored the reprimand, snatched up a cookie, flopped to her back, and, munching, emitted the purring sounds again.

Beside the balsam the man pulled out his kitchen knife. He knelt and decapitated a morel growing from the moist mossy ground.

He knocked the knife against the severed mushroom. Chunks of mushroom and bits of dirt fell. He returned to Grandfather Pine and sat. He brutalized the morel into chunks with the dull knife, lining the shards out on his leg like white ants on a log. He tipped opened the Cheez-It box to his palm, catching a dozen or so crackers. He made tidbit morel and cracker sandwiches. Together the dynamic duo snacked in peace listening to the wind soughing through the highest branches above. Eleanor curled into a ball, stuffing her black nose into her soft belly fur. Burglar nodded off until high in the tree above, Crow warned, "CAW-CAW-CAW!"

The man jerked awake from his nap. He jumped up. Orange cracker dust flew from beard and belly. "Vaminose, El. Vaminose." Eleanor took off running; her humpy-lumpy gait heading north. The burglar grabbed the Cheez-It box and dumped a small pile to the ground. He repacked the booty bag, picked up the propane tank, and, quick like a fox, skittered through the underbrush fast on Eleanor's trail.

Crow hopped down successively thicker pine branches to the last one, thirty feet above the ground. The massive limb was a foot thick and thirty feet long ending in a thick and wide platter of green limbs and needles searching for whatever sunlight filtered through the surrounding hardwood and balsam trees. Crow spread his glistening black wings and lofted to the ground. He raised his black roman beak, gargled once, his black tongue sticking out, before picking up a Cheez-It. Moments later another crow feathered in, landing on delicate toes extended. Wings flapped, birds hopped…a raucous domestic ensued as the attempted murder fought over crackers.

At lawn's edge, a man with white hair yelled, "One of these times your luck will run out and I'll shoot you dead, you bugger!" The man fired a round in the air from his revolver.

Crow and companion each grabbed a final cracker and jumped into the air, cawing alarm as they flew up through the limbs, departing for the safety of the blue sky.

2

The devil's own device chirped on the side table, ending Davecki's dream of carefree flying over the beautiful Brule valley. Eyeing the text through blurred eyes, *answr yer fone doofus,* swam before Davecki's baby blues. He sighed and put the phone down. He levered the recliner from flat to chair and got himself upright like the farmer, outstanding in his field. He rubbed the stubble of his strong jaw line. Was I an eagle? More like a chickadee, he thought. Stanski's "donkey-braying" ringtone heehawed. The phone rattled on the side table. Davecki poked the blessing and curse to speaker. "Whatever it is, the answer is no."

"Sweet. I interrupted a nap, didn't I?"

"Stan, you know I'm retired. Right?"

Patrick Stanski's laughter rasped out of the device, "You just keep living that dream, pal. Duty calls. You're joining me as an official police auxiliary to take a statement from a couple at a cabin on the river who had a break-in. The Hermit of the Brule has struck again."

Davecki rubbed the stiffness at the base of his skull. "Nobody's been able to catch him for years. What makes you think we can?" He grabbed his chin and pulled it far left, ignoring the pain of stretching his sterno muscle out. C1 cracked in response.

"Who said anything about catching him? All we gotta do is file a report so insurance will pay. Though it would be great if the dynamic duo put an end to his reign of terror," Stanski said.

"Reign of terror? He's not exactly Genghis Khan."

"Well, excuse me," Stanski said. "I should have said put an end to his serial petty thefts."

"Petty thefts? Your commitment to the public's safety and security is impressive." Davecki pushed his chin the other direction. No cracking bone sound this time.

"So, there's no winning with you today, then," Stanski said.

"Give me a break. You just woke me up."

"Shake a leg partner. I'm almost at the trailer."

"I haven't eaten, Stan."

"Got you covered, pal. I carry provisions from afar."

"I was an eagle flying over the valley looking down on the river," Davecki said.

"Your grandiosity is showing, pal."

"Well, if makes you any happier, I could have been a chickadee," Davecki said.

"Way happier," Stanski said.

"What's for lunch?" Davecki asked.

"Sophie's smoked fish from Port Wane," Stanski said.

"Sweet. Love it. Be patient, I have to make my afternoon alkaloid."

"Covered. Fresh brewed by lovely Loretta at the store. You owe me twenty bucks," Stanski said.

"Twenty!? No way!" Davecki groused.

"The fish and coffee were ten. All I had was a twenty. I told her you were a big tipper."

"Jerk," Davecki said. He poked *end* but not fast enough to cut off the laughter.

In the Hyundai Ioniq squad, Davecki separated herring flesh from shiny brown skin and delicate bones. He ate. He chewed. He spoke around his food, "Man, this is delicious. Thanks."

"Don't forget the Jackson you owe me," Stanski said.

"Sawbuck, man. I'm not paying for your flirting."

"It's not flirting. It's called being friendly," Stanski said.

"Right." Davecki sipped coffee. "Weird how quiet these electric cars are." He plucked more fish flesh.

"It's a hybrid, not a Tesla, nimrod."

"Picky. Picky," Davecki said.

"I miss having a real squad," Stanski said as the car slithered onto Hayfield County's bumpy blacktop. He slapped his knee to help his foot step on the accelerator. "Pathetic. If this was my Dodge we'd be going a hundred by now."

"How ironic…you…stuck with an Ioniq," Davecki mocked.

"You're not funny. You know that, don't you?"

"So I've been told. You deserve a squad like this, Stan. Hitting a twelve-point buck at a hundred is a big no-no."

"It was only ninety," Stanski defended.

"Ninety then. Either way you shouldn't have been driving that fast for no reason in whitetail country while the rut was on," Davecki said.

Silence threatened to precipitate serious conversation.

Stanski rained on the deep conversation parade, saying, "I hate technology."

"Fleet tracking's here to stay, pal. Your *Top Gun* days of feeling the need for speed are over. Your punishment is the slowest squad in Wisconsin." Davecki snarfed the last of the fish. He wrapped the wrapper around the skeletal remains and stuffed the white wad into the half-full or empty plastic garbage bag hanging from a dash knob.

"At least I'm better looking than Tom Cruise, right?"

Davecki swallowed more coffee, coughed out, "In your dreams."

"Did you hear Stimo Parkinson finally died?" Stanski said.

"Seriously? Too bad. What a waste."

"Too bad doctors didn't believe in Lymes back then," Stanski said. "All they had to do was give him Azlocillin," Stanski said.

"Who would have thought becoming a warden was a death sentence."

"Tell me about it." Stanski picked up the radio mic. "One eighty two...radio."

Dispatch Michelle's voice responded. "Go ahead, Stan."

"Yeah, what was that address again...for the B&E call?"

"You see that computer to your right? It's there for a reason," Michelle's irritated voice echoed from the radio.

"I'm a troglodyte plus I always enjoy hearing your dulcet tones," Stanski said.

"Dulcet? Get real, Stan," Michelle said. "The address is one oh-two-nine-oh East Percival Mine Road."

"Ten four. Car Fiddy-four out," Stanski said into the mic.

"Good one," Michelle said.

"Thanks," Stanski said. He hung up the mic.

"Roger-dodger-dooger-deeger," Michelle responded.

Shaking his head, Davecki asked, "How do you two get away with such shenanigans on the air?"

Stanski huffed. He corner-eyed Davecki, said, "Who's going to care? The Radio Warden in the Sky? Besides, we got a fan base to please out there in Scanner Land. People are listening, don't cha know."

"Your grandiosity is showing," Davecki said.

Two miles east of the river, Stanski turned from U.S. Highway 2 onto Cleverston Road. "Dang! I just washed this thing. Now it's going to get all dirty," Stanski squawked.

"You washed your squad? In Hayfield County? With all its dirt roads?"

"Department policy. Gotta maintain good public appearance," Stanski said. "You never get a second chance to make a first impression."

"Where do you come up with these lines?" Davecki asked.

"It's called reading. You should try it sometime."

"I out-read you ten to one," Davecki said.

"Right. Hear from Hawthorne lately?" Stanski asked.

"She likes Hawaii."

"That's it?" Stanski side-eyed Davecki again.

Davecki looked straight ahead at the dirt road less traveled. "That's it."

At the junction of Cleverton and C-Squared Road, Stanski turned right toward the river. A mile later, a plywood sign the size of a suitcase with hand-painted letters O'GRADY stood. Stanski turned left on to the private two-track lane. The grass growing up from the middle of the lane polished the Ioniq's low-slung undercarriage with the audible swish of tall grass against rolling steel.

"Hope the catalytic converter doesn't start that Mohawk grass on fire," Davecki said.

"There's such a thing as Mohawk grass?" Stanski asked, steering around a muddy pothole.

"It's called a figure of speech. I was referring to the stand-up grass between the ruts."

"Can you even say the word Mohawk anymore?" Stanski asked.

"Who knows? You going to report me to the cancel culture cops?"

"Your secret's safe with me," Stanski smirked.

The enshrouded lane overhung with tall hardwood trees seemed like a tunnel passage. The encroaching honeysuckle, buckthorn, and willow reached out to scratch the squad's clear coat. After a half mile of steady, uphill boonie-bouncing, the brush pulled back like a retracted handshake revealing the O'Grady place.

Stanski executed a whiskey turn in the teardrop turn-around in front of the lovely log home with its shake roof and attached garage.

"Money," Davecki burped.

"What's your first clue?" Stanski asked.

"The fully restored '65 Bronco," Davecki said.

"Interesting plate," Davecki said, nodding at the Minnesota plate O-I-L-I-B-H-E-A-R on the cream colored classic.

"Wonder what that's all about," Stanski asked.

Davecki scanned the building beyond the Bronco. "Place hardly qualifies as a cabin. More like a lodge."

Stanski said, "Cabin on the Brule translates to, we made a fortune elsewhere doing something more important than you."

"Love your sincerity, pal," Davecki said, looking through the squad's side window.

"Nice to be loved," Stanski said.

"There's something you don't see very often," Davecki said, nodding at the man and woman walking across the washed rock path from the cabin to the parking lot.

Stanski put the squad in park. "What?" he asked.

"A tall Irishman," Davecki said.

"Not funny, Mr. Profiler," Stanski eyeballed Davecki as he reached for his N95 mask hanging from the heater control above the plastic garbage bag. "Don't embarrass me, okay?"

"Moi? Embarrass you? Never!" Davecki said. He pulled out his Vikings mask.

"I wish you'd get rid of that purple and gold rag. It's offending me," Stanski said. "Offending someone is a Class D felony these days."

"Guilty as charged," Davecki grinned.

"Just don't embarrass me."

"Misdemeanor embarrassment at most," Davecki laughed.

Outside the squad, from a decent social distance, Stanski asked, "Do you folks want us to wear masks?" He raised the N95 hooked on his thumb.

Davecki, standing outside the squad, twiddled with the Vikings. Looking over the blue car roof, he thought: service revolver, check; Taser, check; handcuffs, check; COVID mask, check, multiple booster shots, check...law enforcement has come to this.

"No need. No need," the man said. "Oliver O'Grady," he added. He stuck his hand out toward Stanski and immediately retracted it. "Such a habit," he said.

Stanski unbuttoned his shirt pocket flap, hooked the mask loop behind the button and reclasped it. He nodded across the car roof, "This is Dave Davecki. He's an auxiliary deputy and a former partner in another life.

"Nice to meet you both," O'Grady said, nodding at the pinicle of rural law enforcement. Snowy-owl tufts of gray/white hair stuck out from under a ball cap with an embroidered badge that said, *IRON CREEK PIZZA.*

Davecki tossed his mask to the car seat. He slammed the car door and walked between the squad and the big boulders lined up like a string of mama bears protecting the lawn. "Nice to meet you, Mr. O'Grady," Davecki said. He extended his hand and retracted it in the new normal greeting ritual.

"Call me Ollie. This is my wife, Sarah," O'Grady said. His entire face lit up around his happy smile. The parchment-like skin of his temples flexed into even more crow's feet. "Sarah is Irish for

Princess," he added, "but really," he looked at her like a devoted Great Pyrenees, "she's my queen."

Mrs. O'Grady's thin lips smiled in an oval Mona Lisa type face. Her black, straight hair hung to the collar of her navy-blue South Face down vest. Faint veins of natural looking gray streaked the silky locks top to bottom. Dancing blue eyes sparkled.

She's a handful, Davecki thought.

Mrs. O'Grady said, "In Hebrew it means noblewoman." She stuck her hand out toward Stanski and retracted it quickly. "Such a habit," she said, her words were tinted with a distinctive Irish brogue.

"What it really means is she's bossy and runs the show," O'Grady grinned.

"Hardly," she said. She elbowed her hubby.

"Nice to meet you, Mrs. O'Grady," Stanski said.

"Call me Sarah, please," she answered. "Thanks for coming," she added.

"Will do. No problem," Stanski said.

"What's your license plate stand for?" Davecki asked.

"It's Gaelic for Oliver," O'Grady said.

Duh, Davecki thought. Should have known.

"Shall we look at the crime scene?"Stanski asked.

"Walk this way," Mr. O'Grady said, turning toward the much-more-than-a-cabin.

Wonder if he's a Mel Brooks fan, Davecki wondered.

Trailing Oliver and his queen, Davecki studied the building. The base course of logs were thick as rain barrels; succeeding courses diminished to the diameter of old fashioned ten gallon milk cans. The chinking here and there was lighter in places where recent repairs had been made. The corner notches showed evidence of hand-hewing. "How old is this place?" Davecki asked.

O'Grady's voice trailed back, "The original cabin was built in the late 1800s; there's been a lot of renovations."

"We've spent a fortune so Ollie could live like Daniel Boone," Queen Sarah said, adding a sing-song laugh.

Daniel Boone never had it so good, Davecki thought.

Mr. Boone Wannabe shot her a glance and clucked without humor.

"Damn fool took the Hillerman I was in the middle of," O'Grady said, walking to the recliner. He picked a bookmark off the side table next to the recliner and twirled it around with twitchy fingers. He sighed.

Parkinson's? Davecki wondered.

"He always takes books," Sarah said. She walked to the dining table across the open-floor-plan room. "He must have taken some time working this puzzle," the Mrs. said. "The Cheez-Its are gone and there's crumbs all over the table and floor."

Moving to the side of the table, Davecki said, "You know what that means," he played his own straight man.

"No. What?" Oliver asked.

Stanski sighed heavily and shook his head.

"You have a really crumby puzzle," Davecki said with a grin and looking at his audience like a failed stand-up comedian.

"Ugh," Sarah said, staring at Davecki.

"Don't mind my partner," Stanski said.

"I won't," Sarah said.

"I think it was funny," Oliver chimed in.

As silence attempted a coup, Sarah foiled the revolt asking, "What's this?" She bent down and picked up a strand of hair. She held the coarse thread of keratin for all to see.

Davecki leaned in. "May I?" he asked reaching for the follicle.

"Feel free," Sarah said, handing the hair over.

Eyeballing the evidence, Davecki pronounced, "Raccoon."

"And you know this how?" Sarah asked.

"You tie flies?" Oliver asked.

"In the winter mostly," Davecki said. He spun the hair between his thumb and forefinger. "It's coarse and variegated."

"Is it okay to clean this?" Sarah asked nodding at the table.

"Knock yourself out," Stanski answered.

She cast a sideways glance at Stanski, extended her palm to Davecki who placed the hair like he was handing out a communion wafer. She moved right into sweeping orange crumbs with her right hand to her left palm held under the table edge.

"Glad he took the whole box," Mr. O'Grady said. "Wouldn't want to be eating after him."

True, Davecki thought. "Anything of high value taken?" he asked.

"My autographed Anne Hillerman was plenty valuable, if you ask me," O'Grady said. "We spent a bundle attending her appearance in Womanotowish last fall."

"Pfft!" Mrs. O'Grady pffted. "He took the usual. Canned goods, batteries and the propane tank from the grill," Mrs. O'Grady said as she walked toward the kitchen with her crumby hand held out like a beggar seeking alms.

Stanski walked to the fireplace mantel where an unholstered single action Ruger .357 magnum revolver lay. Picking up the handgun, Stanski said, "But he left the handgun." He sniffed the barrel. "Smells recently fired. It loaded?"

"Of course it's loaded. Empty guns kill people," the Mr. said. "I fired a warning shot in the air just in case he was hanging around. Want him to know this is serious business."

Any burglary is, Davecki thought. Young people around here have bled to death doing the same, he thought.

Stanski scowled. "You always leave loaded weapons out in the open?"

"An unloaded gun is worthless as teats on a boar," O'Grady said.

"OLIVER!" Mrs. O'Grady yelped as she returned from the kitchen, swiping her hands.

"I'm just telling it like it is. The next most useless thing is keeping it in a gun safe," O'Grady added.

"You're impossible!" Mrs. O'Grady said. "The hermit's not into machismo. He only takes books and canned goods."

"And batteries and propane tanks, and hats," Mr. O'Grady added.

Putting the gun down, Stanski ran his hand along the smooth gray mantel with its meandering black veins looking like old blood vessels. "This is quite the piece of wood."

"Spaulted Maple," Mr. O'Grady said, "Part of the original building."

Mrs. O'Grady said, "We had Nick McNorlen install a deadbolt thinking it would keep him out. But, as the saying goes, when one door closes a window opens."

Mr. O'Grady glanced at his wife, shook his head, said, "Or something like that."

She sounds like Stanski, Davecki thought.

"I told her it was worthless to put a deadbolt in. I said that we should just start leaving peace offerings outside the back door. But nooo."

With your itchy trigger finger, it wuld be more like bait than an offering, Davecki thought.

"Penny wise and pound foolish, that one," the Mrs. nodded at the Mr.

"Why he took my Stormy Kromer hat after winter's done is beyond me. That was my favorite hat," Mr. O'Grady said.

"He took your hat?" Davecki asked. "That's low."

"Tell me about it," O'Grady said. "One of these times he's going to get real unlucky."

"Now, dear," the Mrs. said.

"Where'd he break in?" Stanski asked.

"Kitchen window," O'Grady said.

"Shall we take a look at that?" Stanski asked.

The O'Gradys led the way out back to a neat and tidy woodpile under the two-foot eave. The pile was exceptionally orderly except for some oak and maple firewood scattered on the ground.

Used to be crime scenes had blood spatter, Davecki thought. Now they have firewood scatter.

The bent window screen was propped against the log wall on top of the highest rank of firewood.

"He entered here and left through the front door," O'Grady said.

Captain Obvious, Davecki didn't say.

"Seems like he knows whenever we're away," Mrs. O'Grady said. She picked up a piece of oak, placing it on the pile.

Mr. O'Grady shrugged, "He hits the summer-only cabins in the winter. Easy pickings." He picked up the wood chunk his Queen had just placed and turned it 180 degrees. "People come to open up in the spring, and they've been hit."

"Quit being such a fuss-budget," Mrs. O'Grady said, moving another piece of wood from the ground to the pile. "You're worse than Monk."

"*Your* woodpiles fall over in a light breeze," King O'Grady said.

"Pfft," the Queen pffted.

Davecki looked across the lawn spreading to the north where the dark waters of the Brule flowed past the boathouse. "We should have a look around the perimeter."

"You folks okay with that?" Stanski asked.

"We're fine," Queen said.

"Have at it," King said.

Stanski and Davecki left the O'Gradys wrangling firewood and expectations.

Walking past the pile of Grumman aluminum canoes all hand-painted different bright colors stacked akimbo against the half log siding, Davecki said, "See that green one on the bottom?"

"Yeahhh," Stanski said dragging out his answer.

"That's wooden. It looks like a Henry Denny cedar strip."

"What in the world are you talking about?" Stanski asked.

"Just the oldest hand-built cedar strip canoes on the river. That's all," Davecki said. "They're worth a fortune."

"I thought Lucius had the distinction of being the Cadillac of Canoes," Stanski said.

"Lucius? Who's Lucius?" Davecki asked with a smirk.

"If it's a boathouse, why are the boats outside?"

Davecki shook his head, "Picky picky."

They walked the bank of the north-flowing river to the lawn's edge where it met the phalanx of alders guarding the deeper woods. A big black crow flew by at treetop level and cawed once. They followed the alder formation back toward the house.

"There you go," Davecki said. He stopped walking.

"What?" Stanski asked.

"Bent parnassus," Davecki pointed to the ground.

"Bent what?" Stanski asked.

"You flunk botany class?"

"I acknowledge your superior intellect and superior education. Just talk normal, will you?" Stanski said.

"Bent grass," Davecki said, shaking his head. He pushed an alder branch aside. "Look at that," he pointed to a deep boot impression in the muck of the lawn's perimeter ditch.

"Musta been hauling ass to sink that deep," Stanski said.

"And loaded down to boot," Davecki punned.

"You're a sick individual, Dave."

"Thank you, thank you very much," Davecki did a passable Elvis imitation as he stepped across the ditch into the woods. He let go of the branch and moved deeper into the woods.

"Hey!" Stanski yelped as the branch swung back at his face.

"You snooze, you lose," Davecki laughed.

Fifty yards into the woods, Davecki said, "There you go."

"What?" Stanski asked, looking around Davecki's shoulder.

Davecki stooped to the base of a big white pine tree and picked up a dead, dry, brown popple leaf. He studied the leaf like he was Walt Whitman planning a poem.

"What?" Stanski asked again.

Davecki handed the leaf to Stanski. "These are my friend," he puffed out his chest, "if I'm not mistaken," more chest puffing, "are Cheez-It shards."

Stanski took the leaf. He rubbed orange crumbs off with his other finger. "I'll be."

"Seems like the wascally wabbit doesn't believe in leave no trace," Davecki said. He knelt and picked up a strand of hair. "More raccoon guard hair." From his kneeling position he studied the area. He rose and went to a downed balsam tree laying flat on the ground. He moved some dead leaves aside. "There you go," Davecki said.

"What?" Stanski asked.

"That's a cut-off mushroom stalk," Davecki said. He bent a little closer to the ground and pointed. "Probably a morel. See how the rim of the stalk is crushed and jagged? Definitely been off with a dull knife."

"If the hermit did this, you know what that means don't you?" Stanski said.

"That he likes truffles?"

Stanski smirked, "Well, that too, and he's a fun-gi to be around."

"You're sick, you know that, don't you?"

"So I've been told," Stanski said.

Davecki stood. He looked around the little cove of protection the giant white pine afforded beneath the broad space of its fan-like boughs. He went to the base of the 40-inch-thick tree. "Ah-ha."

"What now?"

Davecki picked up an orange bit the size of a thumbnail. "Cheez-It," he said. He popped the delicacy in his mouth.

"You're eating evidence, hoser."

"Write me up. Sheriff Nottingham will love it," Davecki grinned. He scrubbed his stubbled chin with thumb and finger. He stuck his finger in his mouth. He raised his wet finger to the still air. He raised his nose and sniffed. He swiveled north and west and east.

"So, oh great mountain man, which way did he go?"

Davecki looked long to the west. He raised his eyebrows and said, "That-a-way," he pointed north. "Or maybe that-a-way," he pointed west. "Or…."

"You're no help," Stanski stopped the charade. "Let's get out of here before the mosquitoes discover us."

"Too late," Davecki said, slapping his neck.

They beat feet for the house.

As they gained the lawn, a black-clad man with a gnarly black beard peered around the thick trunk of another nearby pine. The whites of his eyes flashed as he blinked and shook his head and departed in the opposite direction, followed by a raccoon.

The O'Gradys were sipping drinks and sitting on the porch with its bent and twisted cedar balusters looking like gnarled fingers holding up the 2 x 6 cedar balustrade.

"Can I get you some refreshments?" Sarah asked.

That would be nice, Davecki thought.

"No. Thanks," Stanski said. "You can download my report to show the insurance in a couple days." He handed the Mrs. his card. "The website is printed at the bottom."

"For what?" Mr. O'Grady said. "We're not filing a claim. Just makes your rates go up. We just wanted it on the record in hopes that the County would finally do something."

"We're on it," Davecki said.

"Have a nice day," Stanski said.

"Every day's a nice day," Sarah O'Grady said. "Thanks for coming." She lifted her frosted glass in salute.

"Whatever you say, my Queen," Oliver O'Grady said. He inclined his glass toward her. They clinked in agreement.

They've been married a long, long time, Davecki thought.

In the squad, Stanski asked, "When you said we're on it, what exactly did you have in mind?"

"I'm thinking trail cameras."

Stanski said, "Two years ago we put three trail cams up around the Spruce Island RV Park and Campground. He was hitting camper trailers for their propane tanks."

"And...?" Davecki asked.

"He grabbed them all."

"He managed to get all three? Usually camera thieves miss one that gets their picture," Davecki said.

"Not this guy," Stanski said.

"Strikes me as not a real concerted effort to catch him."

"Well, he quit terrorizing Spruce Island, and all it cost was the price of three Cuddebacks."

"That was before wireless," Davecki said. "With Bluetooth units now, they would send the pics before he could disarm them."

"If he's as sneaky as he seems, he'd spot the cameras before they photographed him. Besides, ever since the county lost the twenty-million dollar lawsuit with Coulè Township over that stolen sand, no way will Sheriff Nottingham pay for more cameras, his budget's shot for the decade," Stanski said.

"So, they got found guilty of that, huh," Davecki said.

Stanski sighed, raised his eyebrows, "You oughta know better than that."

"Huh?" Davecki said.

"Government is never guilty of anything," Stanski said.

"No contest then, I take it," Davecki said.

"Exacto-mundo mon frère," Stanski said.

"So, I'm guessing thermal imaging fly-overs by stealth helicopters, ultrasonic seismic sensing, ground-penetrating radar, LiDar, and geo-stationary satellite imaging are non-starters," Davecki said.

"You forgot tracking the vaccination RFID nano-chip signals, but, yeah," Stanski said.

"Umm, just a wild guess, but I'm guessing the Hermit of the Brule is unvaccinated."

"Another charge we can file against him," Stanski said.

Davecki sighed. "Plus, the cell-cam thing wouldn't work around here," he hefted his phone. "There's no signal all along this part of the river. This situation calls for old school methods."

"Such as?" Stanski asked.

"Stake outs," Davecki said. "What you doing this evening?"

"No can do. C.E. training at the jail tonight."

"What class this time?" Davecki asked.

"Whole body listening."

"New Age policing is here to stay," Davecki said. "I'm surprised a defunded department could afford such expensive training."

"Undersheriff Elliot wrote a grant for the money," Stanski said. "Big time facilitator/trainer from Madison getting five grand for a one-night department-wide training."

"Wonder if I could get a grant for freshwater research," Davecki said.

"You're a biologist?" Stanski said. "I never knew."

"I got my PhD in freshwater research on-line," Davecki said. "All my time on the Brule got me tons of curriculum credits."

"Sounds fishy to me," Stanski said.

"Steelhead fishermen all become biologists eventually through dint of their fishing strategies," Davecki said.

"I can never figure out what a steelhead is," Stanski said. "Is it a trout or something else?" he asked.

"I could explain it to you but it would violate the time honored fisherman's code of keeping the public and rank beginner's in the dark," Davecki said.

"Your PhD in BS keeps getting Piled higher and Dryer," Stanski said. He sighed. Shaking his head, he asked, "So, what's the plan Doctor Davecki?"

"I'll go back to the PLS and snoop around for more signs, find a couple of stake-out spots for cornering the guy," Davecki said.

"Good to know. Now I can tell the multi-agency search party to start at the Place Last Seen when we have to come rescue you again," Stanski said.

"Oh I forgot. It's always *my* fault when *you* get *me* into trouble. If you hadn't sent me traipsing off into a blizzard on a cold winter's night everyone could have stayed home nice and cozy," Davecki said.

"You are correct, sir," Stanski said.

Silence intervened with yet another hopeful opportunity for serious conversation.

Stanski staved depth of meaning off by drumming the steering wheel with the fingers of both hands.

"Uh oh," Davecki said.

"What?"

"Whenever you drum your fingers like that, you're thinking something nasty."

Stanski grinned. "Well, maybe not nasty, but…." He went silent.

"Spill, buddy. I can take it."

Stanski said, "Not that I'm suspicious or anything, but something about the O'Grady story smells a little fishy."

"What you got against fish?" Davecki snarked. "What's squonk with them?"

"Not sure. He seems a little too eager with the gunplay talk."

"What's the problem? This is Rittenhous-land man, land shoot first and ask questions later," Davecki said.

"There's that. But, on the one hand they don't seem too bothered by the burglary, frosty drinks in hand and all," Stanski said.

"She's pretty easy going. Keeps him in check," Davecki said.

"Good thing for all concerned," Stanski said.

"So you're saying its overkill with Oliver?" Davecki asked.

"You're a sick individual. You know that, don't you?" Stanski finally said.

"So I've been told."

3

The Hermit of the Brule tossed down a four of hearts. "Fifteen *that,*" he said.

Across the cribbage board in the shape of the perfect hand, 29, Eleanor lay, licking a hard candy. She raised her eyebrows, said nothing, and kept on licking. Hermit picked up Eleanor's cards. He pushed back his new-old Stormy Kromer and studied the cards for a second. He put down an eight of clubs. "Twelve," he said. He picked up his own cards, pulled a three of spades, said, "Fifteen for two." He moved the toothpick in the board five holes forward, putting him three from going out. He picked up Eleanor's cards. He threw down a king of diamonds. "Twenty-five. That was not a smart play, El." He put her cards down and put his six of clubs down. "Thirty one for two. I'm in the stink-hole," he said. "All I gotta do is peg one more, and I win." He looked at Eleanor. She stopped her licking, looked at Hermit, then looked at the board. "But next hand, you count first," he said, gathering the cards to shuffle.

"Ugh," he said. He shifted his behind to the left, letting out a long and loud bottom burp that echoed off the face of the rock wall behind them. He then shifted right and expelled another long and loud burst of air.

Eleanor looked askance at him.

"Shoulda cooked that morel," he said, resuming shuffling and dealing.

The next series of cards gave Eleanor three points. Hermit moved her peg ahead two. "You need thirteen to go out," he said. He picked up her cards, rearranged them with deft fingers. "Fifteen-two. Fifteen-four, a double run of eight gives you twelve," he counted. "That puts you in the stink-hole, too!" Hermit said. "I've got seven," he said, picking up his cards. "I win."

Eleanor said, "Chitter-chit-chit."

"What? Oh, I forgot, you got knobs," he said. "Guess you win after all." He picked up a spiral bound notepad with a battered blue cover, picked up the stub of a pencil and made a mark. "You're two games ahead," he said.

"Chitter-chitter," Eleanor said.

"I agree. Mucho gusto," he answered.

Hermit tipped the two-foot tall and twelve-inch diameter section of white pine log stool he sat on backwards. With one hand he held onto the thick hand-hewn slab of pine tabletop to keep from falling over. With the other hand he reached across the distance to a shelf of granite behind him at arm's length. From the nature-made shelf, he grabbed an open tin can of peach slices in light syrup. He settled back and slurped from the can. He swiped silvery drops of syrup from his mustache. He sucked the sweet liquid from his thumb and forefinger. "You know, El, those guys this morning, especially the one that saw where I got the morel, he could be trouble."

"Chit-chit."

"I know. We'll have to be more careful for a while, until the heat dies down like it always does as summer goes along." Hermit plunked the can down on his table in the wilderness. "Gotta get supper going, don't you think?"

Eleanor finished her candy. She rolled to her back and played with the candy wrapper.

Hermit went to an upside-down 30-gallon plastic tote sitting amongst the array of empty propane tanks, rain-wilted cardboard boxes, a broken aluminum chair, and the various piles of junk he'd gathered over the years from roadsides, cabin robberies, and the detritus of capsized canoes that the mighty Brule caught when disrespectful paddlers didn't tie their gear in. He lifted the gray tote revealing four upturned chrome hubcaps. In each of the hubcaps a mass of slugs congregated for their dinner of stale beer. "Nothing like a good hub cap trap to catch dinner, eh El?"

"Squeak," Eleanor said from the table, still messing with her cellophane.

Hermit picked up one hubcap the diameter of a dinner plate and deep as a pizza box; he tipped it, straining the beer away into the remaining slug traps while blocking with his index finger any of the mollusks from escaping their fate. He kicked the tote back to covering the slug farm. He returned to the table.

Eleanor gave up on the wrapper. She rolled to her side, eyeballing the hubcap. "Chit-chit."

"Just one," Hermit said. He pinched one of the thirty or so slugs from the squirming mass. The snail without a shell clung to the tip of his finger. He extended it toward Eleanor. She extended her front paws and wrapped her fingers around Hermit's finger, bared her white teeth and gently nipped the slug to her mouth. She chewed the treat, she swallowed, she licked her lips, showed white teeth, and pulled on his finger.

"No. I said one," Hermit said.

Eleanor looked up at Hermit. She waved her paws.

"No. I said just one and I meant it. You'll ruin your supper," he said.

"Chit-chit, chitter," she said. She flopped to her side and waved her paws in the air.

"A tantrum won't help your cause," he said.

Hissing, Eleanor quit pawing air, curled in a ball and sulked.

Hermit grabbed a black-bottomed aluminum pot from the backside of the table. He swished all the slugs out of the hubcap into the pot using two fingers. He had to chase one of the more slippery slugs around the under-edge of the hubcap to get it out. In the process the mollusk got mangled. "Okay, El. Here's one more." Hermit flicked the damaged goods to the table top.

Eleanor glanced sideways at the morsel, turned her nose up.

"Be that way," Hermit said. He pinched the unacceptable treat from the table and made a grand display of eating it himself. "YUM," he taunted.

Eleanor glared, her scrunched up black furry mask pinching around beady black eyes.

Hermit stuck the pot under the spigot of a blue plastic jug perched at the far end of the table. He turned the white spigot handle, letting water out. When the pot was three-quarters full he set it on the burner of the green and battered Coleman two burner camp stove. He pumped the brass plunger. He opened the burner valve, stuck a snout-nosed butane lighter under the pot and, "WHUFF," the fire burst to life. Hermit turned the flame down and turned the pot handle inward toward the wind shields. He took a can of green beans from the basalt shelving, opened it with a hand-crank opener, and dumped the entire contents into the pot. From the shelf he plucked a three-inch tall cardboard salt shaker with fall colored leaves decorating the cylinder. He twisted the white plastic top open and shook, shook, shook, salt into the stew. He said, "Time for a nap while that simmers, don't you think?"

"Chitter-chitter," Eleanor said. She gained all fours. She stretched first one rear leg then the other doing her yoga stretches.

"If you must. Just don't go on the blacktop," Hermit said, "or you'll end up as road kill like your mother."

Eleanor glared at Hermit who said, "I know it hurts, just take it as a stern warning that humans driving cars are merciless." Hermit stared back.

Eleanor held the glare long and then blinked first. She moved to the edge of the table. She hooked a front claw in the edge of the plank and executed a twisting-half-gainer over the edge worthy of Greg Louganis. She dangled there showing teeth conveying angst or anger or both.

"Goofball," Hermit said.

"Chittty," she answered and let go, dropping to the ground.

"Be back by supper," Hermit said. "I'm getting my beauty rest." He moved from the rustic table to the back of the deep depression in the basalt face that wasn't quite Bruce Wayne's bat cave. He lowered himself to the foot-high mound of balsam branches upon which lay another foot-high pile of old blankets and comforters. As he ruffled up the top layer of multiple sleeping bags on top of the blankets, he yelled, "Stay off the blacktop!"

"Chitter-chitter," Eleanor said. She shook her head at the immediate snoring. She waddled off toward the east, passing the phalanx of white propane tanks, some rusted, some half buried in the forest floor, heading for the river, and the hope of finding maybe a snack of Purple Wartyback or a slow salamander. No doubt there would be stonefly nymphs under a rock or three.

4

Rolling the squad into metropolitan Iron Creek, Stanski pointed through the windshield. "Will you look at that!"

Davecki looked up from his phone. "What?"

"In front of the IGA," he pointed again, this time with the vigor of an NFL ref pointing out that a Packer fumble recovery had magically transmogrified into an incomplete pass.

"What?" Davecki asked again.

Stanski drove past a jet black and highly polished Ford Expedition with a burnished aluminum trailer attached. The flashers were blinking. "That guy's parked in the no parking zone right in front of the door."

"So?" Davecki asked.

Stanski looked at Davecki askance. "He's breaking the law."

"Big deal. He can move at any time," Davecki said.

"Your dedication to truth and justice is underwhelming," Stanski said. Guiding the Ionic past the Expedition, they observed the male driver bent at the neck studying his phone, oblivious of the passage of law enforcement. At the intersection beyond the IGA Stanski did a Y-turn behind Boyka's Bar, concealing the squad behind the building. He put the squad in park. "I'll give him three minutes as an act of compassion," Stanski said.

"You're all heart," Davecki said.

Stanski lifted his phone. "Hey Siri. Set timer. Five minutes."

"Five minutes counting down now," Siri said.

Without looking at Davecki he said, "Does an additional two minutes of compassion satisfy you?"

In an unprecedented act of supreme self control, Davecki said nothing for half the time allotted. Don't say it, he reprimanded himself.

"This is ridiculous," he failed.

"Chill," Stanski said, grinning. "You got a bladder issue or something?"

"Humph!" Davecki humphed.

Chimes from Stanski's phone announced the beginning of round two. He put the squad in drive and nosed out from behind Boyka's. Both men looked right to see if the violent offender was still making a mockery of society's rule of law.

The Expedition was still flashing and flaunting.

"Guy's got a lot of nerve," Stanski said.

"You need a vacation," Davecki said.

"It's my duty to enforce the law," Stanski said. He parked behind the trailer. He pointed his phone, took a picture of the Minnesota license plate, radioed the number to Dispatch Michelle and said, "I'll be right back."

"Hurry it up. I'm hungry," Davecki said.

"Suffer brother, suffer," Stanski said before slamming the door.

Davecki watched as Stanski stood at the left fender of the trailer writing in his ticket book. He listened to the hollow echo of the shoulder mic transmit the sound of a power window going down. "Excuse me officer. Is there a problem?" a male voice drifted from the driver's side window. The question sounded like it was coming from outer space or the greater Sin Twitties area which amounted to same-same in Davecki's mind.

"No Problem," Stanski's voice came through the radio. "I'll be with you in a sec," he said.

Watching, Davecki heard the driver's side door pop.

"Stay in your vehicle, Sir," Stanski ordered. "I'll be done here in a second."

The door slammed.

Stanski nodded at Davecki.

Davecki shook his head. "Damn fool," he mouthed.

Stanski smirked at Davecki as he tore the ticket from the book. He approached the driver's side of the vehicle. Davecki couldn't see the action, but he could hear via the shoulder mic and knew from experience what the drill was.

"What seems to be the problem, Officer," the male voice asked.

Fair restraint, Davecki thought.

"You're parked in a no parking zone that's also a fire lane, Sir," Stanski said. "This is your ticket. You can pay the hundred-forty-two-dollar fine by check or online at the website printed at the bottom. Have a nice day."

Good even delivery, Davecki thought.

"Hey! Wait a minute! I'm not paying this! It's outrageous! I'm not parked. I'm waiting for my wife. He'll be right out! I've only been here a minute."

"You've been here over five minutes. I timed you for that amount not counting how long you were here before we arrived."

"I'm just waiting. My flashers are on. I can move at a moment's notice," the voice said.

Don't push it, Stan, Davecki thought.

"I assume you turned your emergency flashers on for a reason, sir. Is that correct?"

A pause, then, "Yeah. Why?"

"Turning your flashers on indicates that you were cognizant of your crime," Stanski said.

Cognizant? Crime? Davecki thought.

"Crime?" the man's voice jumped out of the window like a canine officer doing an arm-drag-take-down.

"Are you literate, Sir?" Stanski asked.

"Lord help him," Davecki muttered a prayer.

"Excuse me?" the mail voice squawked a near octave higher.

Escalated, Davecki thought. Stan looking for a fight? He shook his head.

"Would you be willing to read that sign for me, Sir," Stanski asked.

"Who's your supervisor?" the voice asked.

"Sheriff Nottingham," Stanski answered, adding, "That sign says NO PARKING. FIRE LANE."

"The Sheriff of Nottingham?" the voice asked.

Incredulity, Davecki noted.

"Sheriff Wesley Nottingham. He can be reached at the phone number at the bottom of the ticket," Stanski said. "His secretary's name is Robin."

"Seriously?"

"Seriously," Stanski said.

"This is ridiculous," the voice said.

I agree, Davecki thought.

At that moment the sliding glass door of the IGA whooshed open. A portly man dressed in duck brown Carhartt pants, yellow unscuffed boots that looked new, and a spiffy Carhartt jacket topped with a Stormy Kromer hat pushed an extra large grocery cart loaded to overflowing with supplies.

I could use some corn flakes, Davecki thought. Had to take him a while to get that much in his cart, he thought.

"What's your badge number?" the voice asked.

"It's on the ticket," Stanski said.

"My lawyer is going to have your badge," Irate Driver said.

"What's going on, honey?" Cart Pusher asked.

"I'm being shaken down," Irate Driver seethed.

"I told you not to park here," Cart Pusher said, pushing the heavy cart to the back passenger's side door to begin unloading.

"I'm not parked! I'm waiting!" Irritated-To-The-Max man said.

"Unlock the doors," Cart Pusher called out.

The tump of electric door locks reverberated through the squad's speaker.

Cart Pusher flung the Expedition's rear door open, commencing to fling groceries inside with exceptional vigor.

"I assume that, as any reasonably observant driver would, you observed the yellow paint on the curb as you parked," Stanski said.

Stan, Stan, give it a rest, man, Davecki thought. He poked at his phone.

"I'm not parked. I'm waiting," Disgruntled Driver stated.

"Waiting? Is the engine running?" Stanski asked.

"Hey Shelly. Hi," Davecki said into his phone.

The sound of the Navigator's engine starting.

"I'm fine. Thanks for asking," Davecki said. "I'm enjoying watching Stanski make a fool of himself."

"Effin' country bumpkin cops," Disgruntled Driver's voice came through the P.A. system.

"You have a nice rest of your day, sir," Stanski said.

"What you got ready to go?" Davecki said into the phone.

Cart Pusher rushed the empty cart to the cart corral.

"Sweet. I'll take it," Davecki said. "Be there in a few, Shell."

The Expedition's passenger door slammed followed by an urgent, "Let's get out of here, honey."

"I'll have your badge, Officer," Honey said, hostility dripping.

Not, Davecki thought.

Backup lights flashed as the driver put the beastly Expedition in gear.

Stanski stepped back from the driver's window saying, "Court is the first Tuesday of every month if you want to bring it up with Judge Ledeen. Have a nice day, Sir," he added.

Yah right, Davecki thought.

Stanski followed the departure of the cart and carriage, laboring away under its load of rage, groceries, and modern marriage. He turned toward the squad, rubbing his chin and cheeks, trying to obliterate his smile.

Jerk, Davecki thought.

"What was that all about?" Davecki asked as Stanski fell into place behind the wheel.

"It's my 3M policy," Stanski said.

"I'm afraid to ask," Davecki said.

"Make Minnesotan's Miserable," Stanski said.

"And, may I ask, why on earth would you want to do that?" Davecki asked.

Stanski stared forward with a faraway look as if searching for an answer in the distance. "Well, not all Minnesotan's," he said after the potential for seriousness threatened to bloom fully in the squad like a spring flower, "just the ones with entitlement and a bloated ego on such shabby display."

"Whoa!" Davecki said, raising both hands keeping the

ramifications on Stanski's side of the squad. "Way, way above my pay grade," he said.

"Probably a Vikings fan too," Stanski said.

"Well, there's that," Davecki said letting a little of the animus bleed past the laptop consul. "Be that as it may, you were a real jerk. You know that don't you?"

"Takes one to know one," Stanski said.

"I rest my case," Davecki said.

Stanski released the Ionic. It rolled away from the scene of the crime. He stopped at the intersection. The Expedition scrolled past, looking like a slow motion panning shot on a big screen movie. From the still down driver's window the victim's left arm extended, waving the fickle finger of fate.

Stanski snickered.

Before Davecki could comment Dispatcher Michelle interrupted. "One-eighty-two, see the woman, Mercy Madigan, black Tesla, Highway Two canoe landing. Possible assault. Possible robbery."

"Roger," Stanski keyed his mic.

"What? No fancy talk?" Davecki asked.

"Can't overdo it," Stanski said. "Sheriff Wes has his limits."

After the Iron Creek Pizza stop, Stanski floored the Ioniq. "Glacial," he groused.

"Suffer, brother, suffer," Davecki said, around his chewing of the meatball sandwich. His teeth red from Shelly's secret sauce.

"Why didn't you order me one?" Stanski asked.

"You were busy masquerading as a peace officer," Davecki said past the next bite. He held the paper wrapped half-eaten sandwich toward Stanski. "You can have the rest if you want."

"No thanks," Stanski said.

"Suit yourself, brother," Davecki said, taking another chomp.

"Love your loyalty to our lasting friendship, *brother*," Stanski said.

Trying to flog the slow squad down the highway faster, Stanski pushed on the wheel like a polar bear breaking ice.

Davecki swallowed the last of his sustenance. He licked his fingertips clean. "Settle down." He licked some more.

Stanski continued pushing on the steering wheel.

"Breathe" Davecki said, stuffing the sandwich wrapper in the Menard's plastic garbage bag hanging from a dash dial.

Davecki reverted to his phone while Stanski inhaled. Lifting the phone a bit, Davecki said, "Wikipedia says that hermits are usually religious, living prayer-focused lives of seclusion."

"I recall Herman's Hermits being rather public," Stanski said, still bumping the steering wheel, only with less enthusiasm.

"Knock it off with the steering wheel," Davecki said. "It will only go as fast as it will only go."

"It's my penance."

"All kinds of religions have hermits," Davecki said. "I'm thinking our hermit can't be very religious."

"Why's that?" Stanski asked.

"Gee, that's a tough one, Stan. Maybe because he's a serial burglar?"

"Does that mean he only steals Corn Flakes and Wheaties?" Stanski said.

"Not funny," Davecki said.

"Way funny," Stanski said. He huffed, "The biggest thieves in the world are preaching on cable every day."

"Seriously? I thought they were on Wall Street every day," Davecki said.

"Them too," Stanski said. "Televangelists give hedge fund managers a good name."

"You should start a blog exposing all the thieves, scammers, and crooks in the world," Davecki said.

Stanski said, "That's more up your alley."

"Like I have time," Davecki said. "I'm too busy entertaining you and chasing perpetrators of petty theft, as you so eloquently put it."

"I said that?"

"More-or-less. I made it sound more palatable so as to not offend you."

"I'm deeply offended."

"Success at last," Davecki mocked. "Besides," he added, "Exposing crooks and politicians in a blog is a lose-lose situation."

"How so?" Stanski said.

"Making enemies in high places can get you strung up by your shoe laces," Davecki said.

"Like they care," Stanski said. "You know that rhyming for the sake of rhyming doesn't make you a poet, Dave."

"Note to self," Davecki said, "Stan no fun." He turned to his phone screen, scrolling-scrolling-scrolling. He said, "Looks like hermits live in either the relative luxury of a church compound or in mountaintop caves."

"Hmmm," Stanski said.

"I don't know of any caves in the Brule River State Forest. Do you?"

"No. But Warden Wendy would know." Stanski said.

"When you think of it, the Brule Forest is the ideal place for a hermit to hang," Davecki said.

"You're still not a poet," Stanski said, shaking his head. "You've thought about this a lot have you?"

"Only since you dragged me into this," Davecki said. "Think about it. There's tons and tons of wild acreage all along the Brule to stay lost in. There's ample cabins and residences convenient for five-finger shopping and a law enforcement officer with whacko enforcement priorities."

Stanski sighed. "You really know how to hurt a guy."

"You're the one who classifies felony burglary as petty theft and writes punitive parking tickets."

"That's not what hurts so much," Stanski said. "It's your relentless mixed metaphors that cut all the way to the bone."

"Pfft," Davecki pffted.

Stanski slowed the squad for the turn into the Highway 2 canoe landing parking lot. The canoe and kayak rental van was ahead of the squad waiting for an oncoming red pulp truck.

"You should get yourself a soft serve ice cream truck and follow the canoe trailer all day. You'd make a fortune," Stanski chin pointed at the multi-colored rack of canoes on the spindly trailer waiting to turn left.

"That would seriously curtail the lavish personal lifestyle to which I've become accustomed," Davecki said.

"You don't even *have* a lifestyle," Stanski said, following the canoe trailer into the parking lot.

"I'm deeply offended by your implication, to say nothing of your condensation," Davecki said.

Stanski dodged the canoe carrier as it prepared to back up toward the river. "There was no fog this morning, sir."

"Good one Stan, you caught it," Davecki said.

"That *was* pretty good. I give it an eight on the pun scale," Stanski said.

"Clearly a ten," Davecki said as Stanski drove toward a sleek black car at the far end of the lot that was backed into a parking spot. A pair of white legs ending in bright blue water shoes hung out the bottom of a battered red canoe being lifted to the roof.

"Look at that," Stanski said. "She backed into the parking spot. I bet she's Finnish."

"And why?" Davecki asked.

"All the best Finnlanders park their cars pointing out," Stanski said.

"And why do they do that?" Davecki asked.

"Because when the Pinkertons and the FBI show up to split skulls at the Commie gathering, they can make a fast get-away," Stanski explained.

"Clear as mud, Stan."

"You need to read up on local history, man."

"And why would I do that?" Davecki asked.

"Because.... Oh forget it. Just remain ignorant of our area's rich and varied tapestry of important social, cultural, and historical growth," Stanski said.

"Regurgitating lines from promotional fliers doesn't actually make you smart, you know that, don't you, Stan?"

"Smarter than the average bear though," Stanski said.

As the squad approached the Tesla, Davecki leaned forward in the seat to study the situation outside. "Seems odd," he said.

"What?" Stanski asked.

"Loading a fifty-dollar canoe on a hundred and fifty thousand dollar car," Davecki said.

"All the money's going to the car," Stanski said. "Looks like she could use some help; jump out and render assistance. I'll turn around and get the squad in a proper response attitude."

"Proper response attitude?"

"It's in the handbook you were supposed to read. Just get out and help her," Stanski said.

"And be accused of male chauvinism? They want to handle stuff themselves these days," Davecki said.

"They?"

Davecki sighed. "You know. Feminists. Like Hawthorne."

"No wonder she dumped you."

"I dumped her."

"Right," Stanski said, suppressing a grin.

"Quit being mean to me," Davecki said.

"And miss out on all the fun? No way," Stanski said.

"You're all heart, pal," Davecki said.

"Just get out and ask if you can be of any assistance," Stanski said. "It's called being helpful."

"Why do I always have to do the dirty work?" Davecki popped his door.

"Because I outrank you." Stanski let the car roll on.

"Stop already," Davecki yelped.

"Just jump out," Stanski said.

"I'm going to have to kill you, Stan."

Stanski laughed and applied regenerative braking. "Don't forget your mask, hoser."

Davecki was halfway out his door when Stanski let the squad roll forward.

"Jerk," Davecki called out as he danced away from the departing squad. He reached into his Packer hoodie pocket. Laughter echoed within the squad as it rolled away under sufficient power to auto-close the hanging-open passenger door.

"Who you calling a jerk?" the stout woman heaving the canoe to the roof asked. The Styrofoam pads on the gunwales squeaked as she pushed the boat into position atop the Tesla. One of the pads rolled away from the gunwale as she pushed, the sound of the canoe digging a deep gouge in the Tesla's roof made Davecki wince. Reminds me of Mrs. Beakersma, Davecki thought.

"Not you!" Davecki said. Maybe it'll buff out, he thought. He pulled out his Minnesota Vikings purple and gold cloth mask and waved it in the direction of the Ioniq making its whiskey turn at the far end of the parking lot. "My partner's the jerk. Are you Mercy Madigan?" He put his mask on.

The woman's square jawed, un-masked face pinched together. "Who else would I be?"

Ms. Cranky, Davecki thought. "I'm Auxiliary Deputy Dave Davecki, need any help?"

"Sending the B-team, huh," Mercy said.

Merciless, Davecki thought.

"You could help me strap it down." She pried the old red-painted Grumman up with a strong hand and slipped the Styro-pad between the gunwale and the car roof. "Dang," she said. She stuck her thumb in her mouth and put the whetted digit to the scratch and rubbed.

Good luck with that, Davecki thought. Looks to be fifty-ish, he profiled, noting the black nylon holster—empty—contrasting sharply against the khaki clam-digger pants still stained wet in places with river water.

She plucked up a blue dry-bag from the ground. She dug out a *Star Trek* phaser-looking device and thumbed it. The frunk of the Tesla popped. "Thanks for coming," she said.

That's better, Davecki thought.

She pushed the wet looking sleeves of her Stormy Kromer shirt up her arms. She ran both hands through her black hair revealing an earlobe with a hefty diamond stud. A purple bruise the size of an unshelled walnut decorated her high forehead.

Nice shirt, Davecki thought.

Madigan pulled a green nylon device the size of a '60s era walkie-talkie from the frunk. She poked at the device's buttons and clipped it to her belt opposite the empty holster. She pulled a tangle of orange ratchet strap out. Tossing the tangle to Davecki, she said, "Feed this through the other door."

Davecki caught the strapping chaos attempting disentanglement as he walked around the Tesla. He noted the license plate, E-O-G-H-A-N. "What does your plate stand for?" Davecki asked.

Over the roof, Madigan said, "It's Gaelic for Owen."

That sounds familiar, he thought as he imposed order on the straps.

"Toss the hook over," Madigan said.

Resembling Lot's wife after she looked back, Davecki stood there holding the hook end of the strap.

"Hello? You can toss it now," Madigan said.

Snapping back to reality, Davecki said, "Yeah, but I thought the end might hit the car and damage the paint."

"I already damaged the paint. Just toss it over. I'll catch it," Madigan said.

Davecki shrugged and tossed.

The loud clunk on the other side of the canoe generated an, "I said toss, not fast ball!"

Stanski pulled the Ioniq to a stop beside the game of catch or not catch. Davecki watched him mumbling into the mic. When the chrome door handle whispered out of the card's shiny black skin, Davecki thought, cool.

"Hand the ratchet end through the car," Madigan said.

Davecki opened the passenger door and complied.

Stanski finished his status report and got out. He strapped into his

N95. He pulled a green and orange spray can of mosquito repellent from the door pocket. He sprayed as Madigan clicked and clicked the ratchet strap tight.

Davecki went to the front of the car. He whispered, "Cranky."

Madigan secured the load strap pigtail and walked to the front of the car.

"You want some?" he proffered the can toward Madigan.

Madigan waved the offer away saying, "I've got this." She patted the green rectangle strapped to her hip.

"What is that?" Davecki asked.

"It's a Thermacell. It repels mosquitoes. It's got a hundred and ten square foot protection zone so you guys don't need to wreck the environment and your health with that junk." She pulled a coil of blue and yellow paracord from the frunk. Unraveling the tie-down, she worked at snubbing the nose of the canoe to the yellow tow hook protruding from the Tesla's front bumper.

"Does it work?" Davecki asked.

"No, I wear it because it goes well with my shoes. Of course it works," she scowled, "though you're supposed to keep it away from bees."

Not quite the bee's knees then, Davecki thought.

Stanski tossed the dope can to Davecki who caught it and commenced to polluting and ruining his healthy old age. He pointed the nozzle at Stanski and poofed a cloud in the deputy's direction.

Stanski waved at the cloud, flashing a warning glare at the shooter.

A ruby throated hummingbird dove in from out of nowhere like a cruise missle and stopped in mid-air before Davecki's mask, acting now like a USAF drone considering bombing innocents abroad. The menace moved toward the yellow on Davecki's mask like some devious techno-evil from a *Star Wars* movie.

Missing the metaphor, Davecki yelped, "Man, the mosquitoes are getting bigger and bigger every year!" He counterattacked spraying a burst of repellant at the critter.

The bird zipped away toward the river seeking whom it may devour.

Madigan eyed the goings on from a decent social distance. "Why are you wearing masks outside? We're far enough apart."

"Department policy," Stanski said, "unless you don't object."

"I prefer a clear view of your faces," Madigan said.

"No problem," Stanski said. He removed his mask. He unbuttoned his breast pocket. He hung the ear loop around the button and redid the flap.

Davecki set the spray can on the Ioniq's roof. He demasked and stuffed the Vikings into their proper place in the Packer pouch.

"So," Stanski asked, "what happened on the river today?"

Madigan swiped her free palm across the sheen of sweat on her bruised forehead. She winced a little upon touching the bruise. She shrugged. "It was crazy. I read on the paddling forum that Hall Rapids was Class I or less depending on how high the water is. The Internet said the stream-flow was at one-sixty today so I wasn't worried at all. Everything looked cool. Then right in the middle of the fastest water, I drew right but too late. I got sideways, hit a boulder and flipped."

"Bummer," Davecki said. "One person in a river canoe gets tricky at times."

"Captain Obvious," Madigan said, shooting a stern look at Davecki.

Stealing my line, Davecki thought.

Madigan continued, "For a second everything went black. I saw stars. Must have hit my head on the boulder. The water kept me pinned under." Her hand went to her head. She fingered the bruise.

"Helmets are nice," Davecki said.

"Drowning wearing a helmet is still dead," Madigan scowled again.

"No PFD I take it?" Stanski said.

It was Stanski's turn to receive her scowl. "It was in the boat."

The men didn't risk looking at each other.

She went on, "You know it's true that your life flashes before your eyes." She went quiet.

"You were trapped?" Stanski said.

"Under water?" Davecki said.

Madigan snapped out of her reverie and beheld her inquisitors with a broad band of general disregard. She shook her head ever so slightly, and went on, "Next thing I know I felt pulling on the back of my belt. I came up sputtering and blinking as someone dragged me to shore. He dropped me on the bank. I was sort of out of it but heard the holster's rip-stop open and felt him disarming me. I tried to stop him, but he stepped aside and said, 'You don't need this on my river.' Everything was blurry and watery eyed. My contacts were all messed up. It seemed like he threw it into the rapids. At least I heard a splash. Then he took off. All I could see was this black blotch of a guy's back skimming the rapids like a giant water strider. Then he vanished into the brush."

"Huh," Stanski said. "Can you describe the stolen property?"

"A Colt Python," Madigan said. "Chrome plated. Six-inch barrel."

Pricey, Davecki thought.

Stanski pulled his notepad from his breast pocket. His mask fell to the ground. Davecki picked it up while Stanski wrote.

"Was it registered?" Stanski asked.

"No."

"You should've registered it," Davecki said.

"Don't should on me," Madigan replied.

Well excuse me, Davecki didn't say.

"Serial number?" Stanski asked.

"At home," Madigan said. She poked at her phaser again. The trunk lid opened. She picked the double blade paddle off the ground, broke it down, and walked back to put it into the trunk.

"What happened next?" Stanski asked.

She returned and said, "I stumbled downriver, caught the canoe and got my phone out of the dry bag. No signal. I climbed the bank and called. I went back down, found the paddle, and paddled on."

"Why bring a sidearm on a day paddle on the Brule?" Davecki asked.

Madigan glanced at Stanski's sidearm. "Besides being my Second Amendment right, the world is full of crazies. My experience today proves it."

Saving someone's life doesn't seem crazy to me, Davecki thought.

A lingering pause while all present experienced the awkwardness of the new-normal.

She watches too much TV, Davecki thought.

Awkwardness took a step closer to the cliff of real pain.

Or she surfs fake news websites; he followed the thread in his head.

Stanski saved the day, asking, "Anything else?" He took a swing at a superhero mosquito dive bombing through his DEET perimeter.

She asked, "No. That's it. When will your report be available for the insurance claim?"

Stanski nodded, "You'll be able to download it from the county site in a couple days." He pulled a business card from his breast pocket. "Website's at the bottom."

"Thanks," Madigan said. She took the card, shot a snarky glance at them and retreated to her Tesla sanctum sanctorum.

Rolling in the squad, Stanski said, "She seem a little old to be canoeing alone?"

"Agism! Agism!" Davecki chirped like a robin scolding Stanski for being too near her nest.

"It's called an observation," Stanski defended.

"Not anymore," Davecki said. "Now-a-days it's called hate speech."

"I'm just doing my job. Estimating her age is not hating her. I know this for a fact."

"If you say so," Davecki said.

Stanski huffed, "Okay. If it will make you happier, maybe I do hate her. At the whole body listening training the lady called profiling a micro-aggression."

"I rest my case," Davecki said. He laughed. He opened his mouth to stir in his own micro-aggression.

Stanski staved off the attack on his sanity and world view saying, "It's only a misdemeanor."

Another laugh from Davecki who said, "Wouldn't that make a good name for a modern Miss Manner's column? Miss Demeanor?"

"You're not funny," Stanski said.

"So I've been told," Davecki answered. He rubbed his nose, said, "I'm guessing you'll be fired by year's end."

"Not if I retire first," Stanski said.

"Playing right into their hands," Davecki said.

"What's that mean?" Stanski asked, looking sideways at his partner.

"Early retirement is the new code talk for defund the police."

Stanski sighed. The sad slow squad with its quiet ways took over the conversation wielding a hollow silence foreshadowing a bleak future for both of the marginalized creatures huddling in their squad car cocoon. Next, a statute mile intruded, contributing another sixty-seconds of background road noise like a frightened adolescent humming in the dark to keep the bogeymen away. Finally Stanski said, "There's bad cops you know."

"Well aware," Davecki said.

"Wouldn't hurt the situation at all if the bad ones were defunded," Stanski said. He rubbed the back of his neck.

"You did the right thing, Stan," Davecki said.

"I suppose, but squealing on him was one of the hardest things I ever did as a cop." Stanski rubbed his hand over his face.

"When a deputy is the biggest marajuana dealer in the county, somebody's got to stop him. I iterate again, you did the right thing ratting him out," Davecki said.

Stanski glanced at Davecki, smirked a little smirk, said, "Why can't you just say reiterate?"

"Because that would be the department of redundancy department," Davecki smirked his own smirk.

Stanski shook his head. "Your irritation quotient is through the roof."

"Proud of it," Davecki said.

"I suppose the defund the police movement has more merit in urban settings. Things are different out here in the boonies."

"You got that right, pal," Davecki said. "Green acres is the place for me," he half-sang.

"Spare me the singing," Stanski said.

"I'd throw in a little dance with my song, if you had a bigger squad," Davecki said.

Stanski sighed, "All your malarkey aside, Madigan's pretty eager for the report."

"Maybe she's behind on her Tesla payments and needs to scam some insurance money," Davecki said. He poked at the face of his phone.

"Why doesn't the license plate say, Mercy? I bet it's not her car," Stanski said.

"Duh, brilliant deduction, Sherlock," Davecki said. "I bet her Python is tucked away in some secret Tesla compartment waiting to come out and play after the insurance check clears."

"Be hard to deny the claim, with a police report and all," Stanski said.

"True," Davecki said. "If it's unregistered, she could claim she bought a new one if a fraud charge ever arose."

"Fraud charge? Now you're being ridiculous," Stanski said.

"Proud of it," Davecki repeated.

"Though, there's that bruise on her noggin. That's convincing," Stanski said.

"All that proves is she took a blow to the head. Maybe her boyfriend clocked her," Davecki said.

"You're supposed to say domestic partner these days," Stanski said.

"Oh yeah, I forgot," Davecki said. "Maybe it's an SIW." He swiped at his phone's face.

"A what?" Stanski asked.

"SIW. Self-Inflicted Wound. Don't suppose you ever heard of Wilfred Owen," Davecki said.

"Oh yes, my good buddy, Wilfred. What on earth are you talking about?"

"Never mind. Just remain an ignoramus," Davecki said.

"Happy to oblige," Stanski said.

"All joking aside, it's likely she's telling the truth. The bruise, the still wet clothing, the empty holster…I'm buying it," Davecki said.

"Now she's a paragon of truth?" Stanski asked.

"Until proven otherwise," Davecki said.

"Can't argue with that," Stanski said.

Davecki tilted his phone screen toward Stanski. "Looks like an average price for a Python these days is a couple grand; nickel plated are bringing three-gees."

"Like I can see that. I'm driving, doofus."

Davecki said, "Three grand would make a payment or four." He put the phone down and tried to squash a mosquito against the windshield with the back of his hand.

The mosquito bounced to Stanski's side of the windshield.

"Your A.D.D. is working overtime," Stanski said. He reached across the steering wheel and banged his knuckles against the windshield, launching jihad against the elusive bug. "You gotta think it's not her car. Did she look like she could afford a Tesla?"

The mosquito fled back toward Davecki's side.

"Ain't no credit drama, Stan. Most anybody can buy anything they want these days," Davecki said.

"Ten bucks says I'm right."

"No thanks," Davecki said.

"I noticed you didn't exactly make her a lifelong friend with your infinite charm," Stanski added.

"She's the grumpy one. Says more about her than me," Davecki answered.

"Pfft," Stanski pffted.

Davecki smacked at the mosquito again, "Got him!"

"Be proud, man. You triumphed over evil." Stanski picked up his mic.

"One-eighty-two…radio."

"Go ahead."

"Hey Michelle, run Wisconsin plate, E-Eagle, O-Oscar, G-Gary, H-Hammerstein, A-Angel, N-Nicole Kidman's Nose."

"Roger-dodger."

"You guys," Davecki said. "She single?"

"Knock it off," Stanski said.

"Wisconsin plate comes back to Owen O'Grady, 13777 Peter Martin Road, Waino, Wisconsin, no hits."

"You should ask her out," Davecki said.

Stanski shook his head like a horse shaking its bridle. The movement was more of a shudder. "Just quit," he said. "So the Tesla's not her car then."

"Captain Obvious," Davecki said with a grin.

5

As Hermit added water to the slug stew pot, Eleanor returned, a drooping brook trout in her mouth.

"What have we here?" Hermit asked, bending to El's raised offering. "Sweet girl," he said.

"Purrrr," Eleanor said from the back of her throat.

"Did you catch this yourself? Or did rob some fisherman's creel?"

Eleanor spit the fish out and took a little bow, "Chitter-chitter."

"Felicidades. Either way, you did well," Hermit said.

Hermit took the trout to a foot-tall standing block of wood ten inches in diameter on the camp's perimeter. A handsome hatchet stood, chopped into the top like a capital L. He dislodged the hatchet, flopped the fish down, took his Leatherman tool out of his pants pocket and cleaned the fish. He returned to the pot while Eleanor picked through the offal. He used two fingers to sweep away bits of leaves, wood chunks, and slime from the fish flanks. He held the whole fish under the white spigot of the blue water container and rinsed the fish a bit. He rubbed his fingers on the shiny wool of his pants leg, and, with the other hand, dropped the fish whole into the now steaming stew.

"That will take a while," he said. He wiggled the blue water jug. He asked, "Shall we get some water, girl?"

Wiping trout remains from her nose, Eleanor said, "Chit-chit."

"Get the bucket," Hermit said. He grabbed the water jug.

Eleanor scooted under the table, coming out with the white plastic handle of a red plastic bucket in her teeth. Hermit whistled as he walked. He swung the blue water jug like an Easter basket in a young egg hunter's hand. The bottom of Eleanor's bucket bumped along the ground as she followed, head held high.

At the spring at the bottom of the escarpment, Hermit unscrewed the blue jug's white cap that had the spigot in the middle. He knelt on the scrap of plank he'd placed next to the natural spring.

Water surged up from the mossy ground and flowed in a calm steady stream northward. In the depths of the spring water, sand and pebbles rolled and surged like a tempest in a teapot. Eleanor brought her bucket close. Hermit grabbed the white handle. He laid the bucket in the crystal clear water and let it sink of its own lazy accord. As the bucket sank, he reached to the back of Eleanor's head. "Come here, girl."

The tone of his voice made her stiffen. She pushed away, but not in time

Hermit nabbed a pinch of furry nape.

She resisted his pull, front legs straight as daggers stabbing into the moss, rear legs churning against the not so firm firmament of the spongy turf.

Getting her to his lap, he pinned her down and parted the hair at the base of her skull exposing a fat gray engorged tick. "Sorry, I missed one," he said. He pinched the grape-sized tick from her hide. A flake of white-ish flesh dotted the head of the tick. The six black legs wiggled in the air.

Eleanor turned and sniffed the tick.

"Here you go," Hermit said.

Eleanor licked the tick in and bit down. Black blood squirted making her teeth look wicked.

"All better," Hermit said. He let Eleanor go and grabbed the white plastic handle floating on the spring's surface. He pulled up a quart of water and poured a stream toward the opening in the blue jug. Water spattered all around, with the majority of the flow going into the hole.

Eleanor waved her black paws in the air to catch the water splashing. She rubbed her face and hands with the caught water. As she rubbed her ears, glistening droplets of silver water clung to her long white nose whiskers.

Hermit scooped and poured until the four-gallon blue jug was full. They hiked back up the cliff face keeping close to the base of the escarpment, walking on the same exposed rocks used on this and hundreds of other trips, so as to not leave any tracks. At the not-bat-cave, a thick column of steam rose from the pot over the flame. He shut the flame down. He removed the pot. He pulled a battered aluminum 7-inch pie tin from a pile of other tins stacked at the far end of the plank table. Pouring his stew onto the tin, large sections of trout body slipped out of the plate followed by the fish's head, gray shriveled eye staring. Accompanying the fish, blackish-gray dots of tender slugs plopped to the plate. The green beans followed and fell into alignment around the protein.

Hermit grabbed another tin plate from the pile, this one with three compartments. He poured stew into the biggest section and shoved it across the table toward Eleanor, who was waiting with her lower jaw resting on still wet forepaws, claws dug into the table's edge. She rose up and stuck her black nose toward the meal.

"Wait," Hermit said. "Grace!"

Eleanor stared at Hermit, eyebrows scrunched in disregard.

"Heathen," Hermit added.

Eleanor backed away from the stew and stared at Hermit.

"Bless us, oh Lord, for these Thy gifts that we are about to receive from Thy bounty through Christ our Lord, amen."

Eleanor licked her paws. She leaned over her tin and plucked up a chunk of trout, juggling it to cool it.

Hermit spooned up a sampling of the slug stew. He whistled air through his whiskers onto the hot meal. He swept the spoon under his nose that stood out in stark whiteness against the unwashed, hirsute face. He sipped. "Needs more salt," he said. He retrieved the cardboard salt shaker and scattered sodium chloride across his plate. He spooned up another sampling. He blew a couple of times on the spoon and then tipped it to his lips, slugging the slugs down like taking oysters on the half shell.

"Ummm, yummy," he said.

6

Rolling in the squad, Davecki said, "So, the O'Grady's and the Madigan's are connected somehow."

"Either that or she stole a Tesla," Stanski grinned.

"Your blood sugar must be getting low," Davecki said, "you're not thinking straight."

"I do believe you're right. This dire situation calls for one of Grandma Joyce's giant cinnamon rolls at Buster's."

"Too fattening," Davecki said.

"We can split one," Stanski said.

"That never works; we always end up getting a second one," Davecki said.

"That settles it," Stanski said. "Buster's it is."

Davecki sighed. "I suppose."

"That was easy," Stanski said.

Davecki rubbed his chin.

"Uh oh," Stanski said.

"What?"

"Whenever you rub your chin like that some cockamamie plan is hatching."

"Love your confidence in me, brother."

"Well deserved, *brother*." Stanski said. "What you thinking?"

"I'm thinking we should take the metal detector to Hall Rapids and see if we can find that three-fifty-seven."

"Like searching for a needle in a haystack," Stanski said.

"Yeah, but, if we found it we could split the take for fifteen hundred apiece."

"Now who's the unethical deputy, *brother?* We'd have to return it to its rightful owner."

"Why? The salvage law of the sea says finders keepers; losers weepers."

"Nice try, Dave. The Brule is not the ocean. We'd have to return it."

"Stan no fun."

"My middle name is fun," Stanski said. "I've got tomorrow off. We could give it a try." He turned into Buster's parking lot.

"Sweet."

At Buster's the black entry box attached to the door beeped. The red light flashed. "Dang!" Davecki said. He inserted his bright blue vac card in the slot again. The go/no-go box beeped and flashed red again, "Chip must be wearing out."

"Your vaccinations up to date?" Stanski stepped around Davecki at the entry.

"Of course, what kind of public servant you think I am?" Davecki answered.

"I'm not going to answer that," Stanski smirked. He got his wallet out, pulled his plastic vac-card, and stuck it in the slot. The green light flashed. The entry door clicked. "Mine works just fine," he said. He grabbed the pewter colored door handle and pulled.

Davecki made haste to sidestep Stanski and enter first.

Stanski put his free hand out, restraining Davecki. "No you don't, pal. Your vac registration's not in the system. You can't enter."

Davecki shook his head. "First thing I'll do is disarm you. Then I'll shoot you with your own weapon."

"Me thinks thou dost assume too much, mon frère," Stanski said. He laughed and stepped aside, sweeping his hand inward. "Even though you've obviously made it on to the coveted Delta Diner/Amnicon Variants watch list, I'll make an exception in your case."

Davecki snorted away the taunt and brushed past Stanski close enough to make the deputy step back.

They headed for their favorite table in the corner like cows heading for their own personal stalls. Davecki rushed to beat Stanski to the aces and eights chair. They sat. They de-masked.

Her Tiggers mask revealing Buster's zest for high school sports, Arlene arrived, coffee pot in hand. "How's Pete and Repeat today?" she asked.

Davecki, transfixed by his phone, grunted.

Stanski said, "Fine, Arlene. Thanks for asking. Rolls?"

"Coming right up. Did you hear I'm getting married?"

"No. Really? Congrats," Stanski said. "Who's the lucky guy?"

"Fella named Dravecki," she mispronounced Davecki's name. "Nice guy. Lotta money. Kind of a head case at times, but he'll do," Arlene said her sparkling eyes squinched up hinting at the grin behind the mask.

Davecki remained focused on his phone screen.

"You sure you want to take on a head case?" Stanski asked.

"He's old. Got dementia. I'll put him in a home, take his gold. Word on the street is that he's got a mega stash of raw gold. I'll live like a queen off his nest egg."

"Sounds like a good plan," Stanski said.

Arlene shook her head, huffed a little, staring at Davecki who remained transfixed studying his screen, "Rolls coming right up." She hustled to the kitchen.

Stanski watched Davecki scrolling the screen on his phone. "You know," he said, "I'm thinking of busting you for taking those jars of gold from the Harrison case."

"Umm," Davecki said.

"I stole your Amazon Prime password off your counter and ordered a *Game of Thrones* coloring book for you."

"Uh huh," Davecki said while poking and swiping.

"What's so dang interesting?" Stanski moved to grab the phone from Davecki's hand.

"Mine!" Davecki said. He pulled the phone away. In the process he knocked the edge of the table. Coffee spilled.

Arlene returned with the rolls. She plunked the plates down. She pulled the white towel from her shoulder. "You two are always trouble," she said, wiping coffee and staining the white towel brown.

"Is that any way to speak to loyal customers?" Davecki asked.

"Just telling it like it is," Arlene said. She looked across the room as the entry door opened. Two people walked in.

"Interesting," Davecki said, looking past Stanski.

Stanski turned to follow the gaze.

Mercy Madigan and a man stood reading the menu written in

red marker on the white board on the wall. The man was shorter than Mercy Madigan, about the same age, with close-cropped, light colored hair that used to be brownish but was now running heavily to gray.

Davecki raised his hand, waved, called out, "Care to join us?"

"Sure," Madigan said.

The man cast a sideways glance at her.

Davecki scooted to the chair closer to the window. Stanski did the same.

Sitting down, the newcomers removed their masks as Arlene said, "Gotta run your cards."

"We got in didn't we?" Mercy Madigan said.

"Yes, indeedy you did," Arlene said. "Nevertheless, I'm compelled to run 'em by order of state and federal authorities of infinite wisdom."

Madigan and the man produced their bright blue vac cards. Arlene lifted the bright blue card reader hanging from her belt.

Reminds me of Madigan's Thermacell, Davecki thought.

Arlene stuck the vac cards one at a time in the device slot. Each time, the blue box beeped. The green light flashed. "All-righty then, what'll you two have to drink?" Arlene asked.

"Coffee," the man said.

"Chocolate milk," Madigan said.

"Coming right up," Arlene said.

"Fancy meeting you here again so soon," Madigan said. "This is my brother Owen O'Grady."

That explains the license plate, Davecki thought.

"Nice to meet you," Owen said. He initiated a handshake but curbed his intent.

"Same here," Stanski said, nodding.

"Yup," Davecki said. "You two are brother and sister?"

"Sort of," Owen said.

A short pause entered the fray as everyone looked everywhere but at the elephant in the living room.

Mercy rescued the moment saying, "It's a long story."

It always is, Davecki thought.

"Here you go," Arlene said. She set coffee down. She set a tall glass of white milk down.

Madigan's face skewered into a pre-complaint.

Like pulling a rabbit out of a hat, Arlene pulled a squeeze bottle of Nestlé's syrup from her apron pocket. "Best if you mix your own."

Face relaxing to a smile, Madigan said, "Thanks."

"Two of those," Owen said, his eyes bulging at the sight of the huge pastries.

"Coming right up."

"What's the short version?" Davecki asked, looking at Mercy.

Mercy looked at Owen.

Owen looked at Mercy. "You go," he said. "You don't like my version."

Squirting chocolate into her glass, Mercy said, "The sad part is, my parents and real brother were killed in a car accident when I was three. I was visiting cousin Owen here at the time. The happy part is Aunt Sarah and Uncle Ollie took me in."

"Sorry for your troubles," Davecki said.

"Me, too," Mercy said, stirring, stirring, stirring.

"They didn't adopt you?" Stanski asked. He sipped coffee.

"No," Owen answered for his sort-of sister.

Mercy shot him a look, said, "Mom, Aunt Sarah mom that is, wanted me to keep the Madigan name. She says she wished she'd kept her name when she got married."

"Dad loved that," Owen said, rolling his eyes.

Yet another uncomfortable silence ensued.

Arlene rescued the perishing by rushing two more, huge, white frosted cinnamon rolls to the table. "Here you go! Granny Joyce's secret recipe!"

"Thanks," everyone said.

Forks and knives came out as each combatant fought for ways to dissect the four inch square and two inch tall pastries. Davecki swiped the gooey white frosting aside with his butter knife and commenced to sawing into the soft dough. "What's the rest of the story?" he imitated Paul Harvey.

The siblings didn't look at one another as they contended with their hefty treats. Owen shrugged a little shrug. Mercy made a similar gesture and said, "We're having a sort-of family reunion."

Here we go, Davecki thought. He snuck a glance at Stanski who did not return the look.

"I've been away for a while," Mercy said.

"Twenty-five years is more than a while," Owen said.

Dirty laundry day, Davecki thought.

"I had my reasons," Mercy said. She stabbed another piece of roll with her fork and popped it in her mouth.

"After all they did for you," Owen said.

Madigan spoke around her food, "Give me a break."

Oh good, a family fight, Davecki thought. Nothing like a good sibling brawl to get the truth out. The only thing missing is the alcohol. He looked at Stanski, who masticated mightily, still wisely refusing to return the glance.

"Not even a Christmas card," O'Grady said.

"I didn't see you making any grand overtures my way," Madigan said.

"I was too busy caring for my elderly parents," O'Grady said.

They seem pretty competent to me, Davecki thought.

"More like the other way around," Mercy said.

"So…nice that the Packer's beat the Vikings agains, huh?" Stanski said.

The fight was on in earnest as brother and sister ignored the comment, the brother saying, "They should have left you to rot in that trailer in Gurley."

Ouch, Davecki thought.

"Your concern for me is astonishing," Mercy-less said.

"I'm more concerned for them," Owen said.

"I'm forever grateful to them," true-Mercy resurfaced.

"You should be," Owen said.

Rational-Mercy replied, "The Lord provided them when Mom

and Dad died. And He provided them again when I needed help in Gurley."

"You can't compare the two," Owen said.

"They did what they wanted to do. I'm not forever obligated. I don't owe them my life."

"Yes, you do," Owen said.

The heat at the table got doused considerably when Arlene returned. "I don't suppose Mr. Generosity there is buying," she indicated Davecki. "How many checks?"

"I'll get it all," O'Grady blurted.

"No. No. No," three people answered.

"Here's my Visa," O'Grady said over the objections as he pulled out his wallet.

Arlene took the plastic and headed for the Square terminal.

"What happened in Gurley?" Davecki asked.

Stanski looked askance at his inquisitive partner.

"None of your business," Mercy said.

"She got knocked-up. Her loser boyfriend Robby ditched her with no money and three month's rent due."

"Owen!" Mercy said.

Shades of Sarah stifling Ollie, Davecki thought.

"I had a good gig folding napkins at home for MacBrightten," Mercy said.

"Like that was paying the bills," Owen said.

"I could fold five-thousand napkins a day," Mercy said.

"And that made you how much?" Owen snarked.

"Fifty dollars cash money seven days a week," Mercy defended.

"And the MCP joint surgery cost how much?"

Mercy stared hard at her newly nasty brother. "The bill came to almost a hundred thousand, but the county paid for it."

"I rest my case," Owen said.

Sounds familiar, Davecki thought.

Mercy, however, wasn't interesting in resting her case. "I was making good money making wreaths for Hotsy and cleaning for the nuns. I could have made it. If I hadn't miscarried, mom and dad wouldn't have come."

"I noticed you didn't exactly send them away when they showed up at your door."

"They insisted."

"I guess," Owen said. He put his knife and fork down, roll finished. He sipped coffee.

He's gracious in defeat, Davecki thought.

"Sorry about this," Mercy said, looking at Stanski and Davecki. "The only family feuds people like is with Steve Harvey, Owen," she shot her brother a look.

So there is a sense of humor in there somewhere, Davecki thought.

Owen shook his head, said, "I apologize. It just springs to the surface. I deal with it badly. I apologize."

Two apologies is better than one, I guess, Davecki thought.

"No need to apologize," Stanski said. "Family stuff's tough to deal with."

Shut up, Stan, Davecki thought, things were getting interesting.

"When's the County going to do something about the Hermit of the Brule burglaries?" Owen asked.

Sounds like his father, Davecki thought.

"We're on it," Stanski said.

Sounds like me, Davecki thought.

"What are you going to do?" Mercy asked.

"We're going undercover so to speak," Stanski said.

"What's that mean?' Owen asked.

"We're going to do some stake outs once Dave here scouts the best places."

"How you going to determine that?" Owen asked. He looked directly at Davecki.

"I'll go back to the area around your folks' place and see if I can find any tracks or sign of where he might have headed to his hermitage," Davecki said.

"He's been getting away with it for years," Owen said. "What makes you think these robberies will be any different?"

"He's never had the dynamic duo on his trail before," Davecki said.

"Well, good luck with that," Owen said. He finished his coffee and stood. Mercy swigged her milk. They left with Owen stopping at the pay station to pick up his receipt and card.

"That was a fast getaway," Stanski said.

"Hope he left a big tip," Davecki said.

"Irregardless, you're leaving more," Stanski said. "Don't forget," he added, "you still owe me for Sophie's smoked fish."

"If it makes you feel any better, I'll leave a dollar," Davecki said.

"Don't be a cheapskate," Stanski said, "make it two. I gotta use the john."

In the Ioniq, on the way to Davecki's trailer, he asked, "Why'd you stop them from fighting? Things were getting interesting."

"I'm sick of domestic squabbles," Stanski said with Crinkle Face.

"Sucks to be you, man."

Stanski said nothing.

Davecki said, "Irregardless isn't a word you know."

"Is too," Stanski said.

Davecki pulled out his phone. "Dang! No signal."

"Asking Siri won't help," Stanski said. "I'm right and you're wrong," he said, snorting a little laugh. He added, "As usual."

"Jerk."

At the trailer, being dropped off, Davecki said, "See you in the morning. I'll have the canoe in the pickup and meet you at the Highway Two landing to drop the shuttle car. Don't forget to grab the County's metal detector. I'll be there at nine."

"Right on, Saigon," Stanski said.

Alone in the trailer, Davecki said, "Hey Siri. Send a text to Brekken Hawthorne."

"What do you want to say?"

"Hi. Just checking in. Hope things are going well. All good here."

Siri repeated the message, said, "Ready to send it?"

Davecki stared out the window. He set the phone down, went to the fridge, opened the freezer and pulled out a white wrapped package with *BACKSTRAP* hand-scrawled in black marker on the bright white freezer paper. He put the package in the refrigerator. He left the phone on the counter. He headed for the sauna to build a fire.

7

The Devil's own device danced on the kitchen counter like spittle on a hot griddle. Davecki quit stirring his scrambled eggs infused with tapioca pearls and diced pepper-jack cheese. He picked up the phone, read the text from Stanski: *no can do today call out to accident on tickle belly hill.*

"Bummer," he said, returning to the eggs. The toaster popped two slices of sourdough. He spooned maple syrup on the toast, giving it a good soak. He buttered. He peanut buttered. He scooped eggs to plate and carried same with tea to table. He sat. He prayed. "Our Father who art in heaven thank you for this food today please protect me from myself and the devil for thine is the kingdom and the power and the glory amen." He ate. Through the bay window he watched chickadees flitting from the bird feeder to the broken branch where the tallow holder had hung all winter. It was gone now thanks to Blackie the Bear's ritual spring visit and vandalism. Though it was nice to see her and her cubs after the long winter. He picked up his clean plate and half-full or empty cup of Smallenhi green tea, dropping the breakfast detritus on the counter next to the sink. He went outside. He unloaded the canoe and drove to the O'Grady place on the river.

Sitting in the O'Grady driveway, Davecki stuffed a water bottle into one pocket of his fishing vest. In the other pocket, the most valuable northern Wisconsin survival item of all, a spray can of mosquito dope. He unplugged his cell phone from the charger cord. He grabbed two Unkind bars off the seat, inserting them in the breast pocket where the lure case normally went. In the bigger slash pocket he stuffed two strips of Hank Lank's venison jerky fresh from Hank's smokehouse hidden in the hinterlands of Covertland Township. He said, "Hey Siri, send a text to Brekken Hawthorne."

"What do you want to say?" Siri asked.

"Hi. Hope things are going well. Just wanted to say that life doesn't have to be perfect to be great. Bye," Davecki answered.

"Your messages says hi hope things are going well just wanted to say that life doesn't have to be perfect to be great bye ready to send it?" Siri answered.

Oliver O'Grady came out of his Daniel Boone wannabe cabin.

Davecki looked at the phone. No signal. He stuffed the phone in his pocket. He rolled his window down as O'Grady approached. Should trade this thing in for one with power windows, he thought.

"What's up," O'Grady asked.

"Wondering if I can leave the truck here while I snoop around for hermit tracks," Davecki asked.

"How odd," O'Grady said, "somebody doing something about it."

Your gratitude is underwhelming, Davecki didn't say.

"Have at it," O'Grady said.

"Might be a while," Davecki said.

"Take as long as you like. Sarah and I are going to a doctor's appointment. The kids are still sleeping or surfing or whatever they do nowadays, squirreled away in their rooms."

"Thanks," Davecki said. Like a good Finnlander or a deputy who had read the manual, he backed the F-150 between the Tesla and Bronco, *their* noses pointing in.

At lawn's edge where the broken Parnassus and boot mark marked the thief's prior passing, Davecki pulled his white socks further up from the top of his Blackwing boot tops. He stuffed his pant legs inside the socks against the threat of ticks. Cutting for sign from the morel stalk under Grandfather Pine, Davecki found occasional heel marks in the duff, the occasional raccoon print in mud. Noting the short strides, he thought, leisurely pace.

At one heel mark, he stepped in the duff beside the Hermit's print mark. Davecki's heel impression was about the same depth.

Weighs about 180 like me, he registered. Or, actually, less, if he's loaded down with propane and groceries.

Following the occasional heel impressions and the bent fern here and there, Davecki managed to establish a continuity of trail that led to a rivulet tributary cutting down through a steep embankment. I think this is Folidnil Creek, he guessed. At the bottom of the ravine, small boulders varying in size from toolbox to coffee table, held a long dead, twenty-foot-long balsam tree crosswise to the brisk flow of spring run-off water. Behind the half-submerged dead tree, twigs, clumps of dead leaves, and various broken branches made a natural dam in the cut, forming a pool of water the size of a spacious living room. Slithering silver snakes of glossy water wove between the rocks as the water slipped toward the Brule beyond. The bare-backed rocks provided a trackless crossing. After many patient passes up, down, and all around both sides of the creek, Davecki picked up no spoor whatsoever. The elusive hermit had used the bare rock-tops to evade detection.

Forsaking tracking, Davecki lifted his eyes unto the hills and climbed. Atop the ridge he scouted south and north, looking for suitable stakeout spots. Mother Nature must have rung the recess bell, setting the mosquitoes free from blood sucking school to come out and play. He sprayed and the cloud of bugs retreated, but not far, hovering and humming their irritation at hot-blood-lunch denied. Maybe I should get one of those Thermacell thingys, he thought. The poor bees, he thought.

Davecki found a vantage point where the Brule below was visible through the still developing foliage of late spring. At his back, an outcropping of black basalt the size of a house. He placed buttocks on the ground and leaned back against a windfall popple at the base of the rock wall. He pulled an Unkind bar out and munched while surveying the broad slope declining through the trees. The spring foliage was budding, but not sufficiently developed to obstruct his view. A narrow slice of the Brule below took a turn through his field of vision. The mosquitoes hummed patiently awaiting the fall of the repellant wall. The air was still. The sleepy forest had nothing to say. He slumped against the popple. He did what Davecki does best. He dozed into a peaceful nap.

"Ugh!" he said, snapping awake. He reached to his jowl and

plucked a wood tick from its scuttle toward his hairline. "Little bugger," he muttered.

Pinching the pest between thumb and fingernail, Davecki tossed the bug aside and plucked another from his neck. He flicked this tick away. "Good Lord!" he yelped looking at his lap. An army of ticks crawled like a living carpet up both pant legs. He jumped up and took to swatting ticks away. Then he saw yet more ticks on his shirtsleeve and vest.

"Arrgh!" he yelled, looking where he had sat. The ground moved like brown water simmering. He jerked off his fisherman's vest. He swatted it against the nearest popple tree. Ticks flew off like raisins doing back flips into oatmeal. Dropping the vest, he unbuttoned his shirt and spread the flaps. A dozen ticks were square dancing the dosie-doe on the white of his undershirt. "Ugh!" He took off stumbling as fast as he could down the steep incline toward the river below.

As the bug-infested Davecki careened downhill, Hermit and Eleanor, at the brink of the outcropping above, grinned like banshees. Hermit's teeth glowed like a hundred watt bulb in the middle of his hairy face and beard. Eleanor's pointy white incisors may have indicated joy, or evil. "That's what you get for not looking where you're sitting down, eh, El," Hermit said. "If he drank fiddlehead fern tea every morning like us, the ticks wouldn't bother him."

"Chitter-chit," Eleanor agreed.

"At least he didn't sit on a ground wasp nest," Hermit said. Up from the ground he arouse, saying, "Let's roll, compadre."

The talking heads vanished from the precipice. Moments later man and raccoon hustled around the basalt. Hermit leaned down to examine the ground below the popple bench Davecki had leaned against. He picked up a stick and poked at a cluster of tiny orange-ish eggs on a leaf. "Yup, tick nest," he said. The swarm of ticks undulated on surrounding grass and leaves. "Sucks to be him," Hermit said.

"Hiss-hissa," Eleanor said.

Hermit picked up Davecki's vest, shook it. A trickle of ticks fell to the ground. He swung the vest, whacking it against the popple. More ticks flew off. "We'll get the rest later," Hermit said. "For now, shall we gather at the river? The beautiful, the beautiful river?"

Eleanor was already on her way to the big show below.

The sandy beaches of the Brule are tiny but frequent, cuddling up to the inside elbows of the many curves that make up the myriad fishing holes from source to mouth. There are 119 named holes between Highway 2 and the mouth alone. Naked Davecki crawled out of the river shivering and shaking. Dripping, he weaved across the sand to the grassy berm where his clothes lay scattered about. He picked up his Brule Beer t-shirt. He inverted it, looking for ticks hiding in the seams. He pinched a black dot from the seam of the collar. He walked back to the river. He flicked the tick in the water. He shuddered. He inverted the shirt again. He spun it around in the warming sunlight. He picked two more ticks off the seams of the shirt, flicked and returned to the bank. He laid the shirt over the grassy berm like a beach towel and sat on it. He examined his legs. He found a tick and pinched it and tossed the carcass to the sand. He twisted his legs around as best he could to pluck what nasty bugs he could see. He stood. He examined the remaining parts of his body that were examinable. Three more ticks.

Probably a dozen on my back, he thought.

He leaned over. He grabbed his undies. The exam produced two ticks running for their lives across the white cotton fabric and one tucked into the fold of the barn door. Eradicating the vermin, he stepped into the tighty-whities. The clunk of wood paddle against aluminum made him sit down fast.

Around the bend, a battered aluminum Grumman painted red appeared, piloted by Mercy Madigan. "What in God's name are you doing?" she said as she back paddled her craft, nosing the stern into the sandy beach.

Davecki put his elbows on his knees. He shook his head, said, "Delousing."

Madigan jabbed her paddle into the sand and sat, amazement on her face. "Delousing?"

"I sat in a tick's nest up on the ridge and got covered," he said. "Did you know there's a lake out south that used to be called Pesthouse Lake?"

"Seriously?" Mercy said.

"Yeah, it's where all the lumberjacks went for delousing in the spring after a winter of logging and living in harmony with their lice and other vermin."

"Yuk," Mercy said.

"When people started building their McMansions on the shores it was too unsavory a name so they changed it to Lake Mystique," Davecki volunteered. He asked, "You always paddle alone?"

"Owen said he'd come along but he's too lazy. He said he'd pick me up."

What's she really doing out here? Davecki wondered. He picked up his shirt and searched. Pinching and flicking tick after tick to the sand he said, "I've gotten over a hundred off me so far. No telling how many are on my pants and socks and boots and back."

"I'll check your back," Madigan said, de-canoeing.

"Umm.... I...."

"I'm a nurse. I've seen worse." Madigan shipped her paddle.

"The cold bath probably got them all," he said. "Thanks, but no need."

Not responding to his repudiation, she pulled the Grumman more ashore and, crossing the sand, said, "Stand up and turn around."

"Nice to see you're unarmed," he said as she walked toward him.

"Not by choice," she said.

He stood and turned away. Looking at the woods rising to the ridge above, he shivered at her touch as she plucked a tick from the middle of his back. The hypothermia from the dip in the freezing water transformed into heat as her fingers nipped twice between scapula and twice at his hairline nabbing four more ticks.

"Turn around and bend over so I can check your head."

Good doggie Davecki obeyed.

"Man, you have thick hair," she said. She scratched and swept like a minesweeper, picking ticks and tossing them to the sand.

"Are you killing them?" Davecki asked.

"Of course."

Hope they're dead, he thought.

"I think you're good." She patted him on the shoulder. "You always get into these fine messes?"

"No," he lied.

He turned around. He sat and draped his Stormy Kromer shirt over his knees. He picked up a white sock, nabbing another tick looking like a flyspeck on the cotton.

Madigan sat on the berm that was more like a park bench now. She grabbed Davecki's pants and started looking for ticks. Picking, pinching, flicking, she said, "It's hard to believe that so many wood ticks can be in one place at one time."

"I'm trying to keep track. Count how many," Davecki said.

"Oh fudge! I..." she paused. "I wasn't counting. I think it must have been a dozen or so, so far."

"That'll do, keep track from there, if you would, please," Davecki said, inverting a second sock. "No telling how many my skinny dip washed away."

"How could you stand jumping in that cold water?"

"The alternative was worse."

"Such as?"

"Lymes and an early horrible death."

"Lymes isn't fatal."

"Tell that to Stimo."

Madigan scrunched up her face. "Stimo?"

"A friend of ours was a warden for the DNR. Stimo Parkinson. He just passed away from untreated Lymes," Davecki said.

"Really? I'm so sorry. Why didn't he get antibiotics?"

"He got infected early on, before the medical deities admitted there even was such a thing as Lymes."

"Medical deities?"

"MDs, doctors," Davecki said. He glanced at Madigan, "Uh, sorry."

"Some of 'em are pretty bigheaded, especially the old farts," she said. "But the young ones seem more humble and humane, especially the women docs; they seem more level headed...for the most part."

"I'm up to two hundred thirty-seven," Davecki said.

"Twenty-four for me," Madigan said. She rustled the pants around. She pulled the brown leather belt from the loops. "I'd wash these right away when you get home and toss them in the dryer," she said as she twisted the belt loops back looking for bugs in all the right places. "They don't like heat."

"You seem to know a lot about ticks," Davecki glanced sideways at her.

"We had in-service classes in Denver. Rocky Mountain Spotted Fever there."

"Did they tell you Lyme's is a World War II bioweapon experiment gone bad?" Davecki asked.

"You one of those conspiracy nut jobs?" Madigan asked.

"That's one way of putting it," Davecki said. "I prefer to couch in in terms of being a critical thinker open to all sides of a story."

"And to what side are you referring?" Madigan asked.

"It's not unreasonable to think that Lymes is the original Wu-Flu," Davecki said.

"One man's reasonable is another's insanity," Madigan countered.

I wonder why she never answers a question directly, Davecki thought.

She handed him his pants.

Davecki set the socks aside. He leaned forward. He lifted his foot and brushed sand off.

Swishing sand, he said, "The weaponized wood ticks escaped a government lab on an island just off shore from Lyme Connecticut."

"Seriously?" Mercy said.

"Allegedly," he said as he de-sanded the left foot that he'd almost lost due to frostbite chasing Harrison. Putting his pants on one leg at a time like everyone else he said, "You ever hear of the CCCs?"

"Who hasn't?" Madigan said.

Snarky as Stanski, Davecki didn't say. "There was a CCC camp just south of Brule. All those young bucks would walk to town on Saturday night for dances."

"Where is this going?" Madigan asked.

Buttoning his shirt, he said, "The local girls at the dances called the CCC guys, Wood Ticks."

"Your proclivity for the arcane is impressive," Madigan said.

"Thank you. Thank you very much," Davecki did Elvis. He added, "Seems like your family story is pretty complicated."

Madigan picked a crawling tick from her knee. "Oh, fudge! Now I'm feeling all creepy and crawly." She pinched and flicked the tick to the Flanders field below. She looked at the Grumman. "I should get going. Owen said he'd pick me up at Pine Tree at three."

"He's picking you up? Seems like you two don't get along," Davecki said.

"It's a brother-sister act. It's how we relate. He's okay. I caused him a lot of trouble back in the day." She paused, added, "Before I got my act together."

"How about I paddle down the rest of the way with you? That way I can get back to my truck. It would be fun to get a ride in his Tesla. I'm sorta done with ticks for the moment."

"Fine by me," Madigan said. "But I only have one paddle."

"You know what that means don't you?"

Madigan, starting for the Grumman, said, "No."

"I'm up the creek without a paddle," Davecki said.

"You know you're a sick person, right?" Madigan quipped.

"So I've been told."

Madigan sighed and, as she bent to her boat, said, "Now I know why Oliver always harassed us about bringing an extra paddle." She handed her paddle to Davecki. "You know what this means?" she asked.

"No, I don't."

"You're going to paddle me down the river like the Queen of Sheba. I'm going to sit back and enjoy the ride."

Davecki took the old wooden five-footer with a crack in the beavertail and little woody hairs sticking out the blade tip from years of striking the Brule's rocky bottom. He helped Madigan scrape the boat back into the water. She got in. He got in. They got going.

Another fine mess you've gotten me into Ollie, Davecki thought. Next he thought, it's a wonder she's back on the river so soon after nearly drowning.

Watching from the concealment of the brushy bank as Davecki paddled his not-African-queen away, Hermit said, "He forgot his vest, El."

Eleanor looked up from ripping open the last Unkind bar package and grinned.

8

Like the Hopeless Diamond, the Bois Brule has many facets and only the occasional curse. Every now and then a beaver will kill a paddler or a Brule Valley farmer will put a lit stick of dynamite under his hat and patiently await his fate, but, for the most part the facets shine; from whopping whitewater to righteous riffle to placid oxbows, the river reflects the myriad hypnotizing charms of the jewel it is. Of course there's the growth opportunity of dragging a heavily loaded canoe across Miguel Saari Flats where a toy plastic boat wouldn't float. The Meadows Section meanders its scenic, quiet, and—truth be known, boring—beauty, the polar opposite of Skid May's adrenaline junky ledges. What wasn't boring to Davecki was his passenger.

Her Majesty Queen Mercy Madigan of the Brule sat on her old orange life vest throne insulating her bottom from the hard cold aluminum hull. Her arms akimbo on both gunwales and leaning back against the thwart, her face tipped back in reverence to the mild sunlight, she closed her eyes and said, "This is the way to paddle the river."

Except you're not paddling, Davecki didn't say.

"If we had grapes, I'd ask you to peel me a grape, man-slave," Mercy said.

Looking around, Davecki thought, good thing cancel culture's not rampant in the semi-wilderness. Here's hoping Warden Wendy doesn't appear, me without a PFD, he thought some more.

Mercy rocked the boat, rolling the sleeves of her tee way back toward her neck, exposing white skin. "Good to get some sun on my shoulders," she said.

Sunshine on her shoulders makes her happy, Davecki thought of John Denver and his last not-canoe ride.

Madigan leaned back again, "This is nice."

"So, I take it you've had more than your fair share of troubles in life. How'd you get straightened out?" Davecki asked.

"Oh, look!" she said, pointing up at the broad band of blue sky retracting the crowding evergreens like Moses parting the waters.

Davecki looked up in time to catch the stoop of a bald eagle heading to flat water ahead. The baldy dove, glided, reached out, reached out and, deadly talons touched an unwary brook trout. Careening up from its fishing run, a twitching trout flashing sunlight in its talons, the eagle disappeared around a bend in the river. "Awesome," he said.

"No kidding," Madigan shifted around on the boat bottom, leaning back further in her royal—or not—repose. "Have you ever seen anything so majestic and beautiful?"

"Seeing any wild animal in action is always impressive," he answered.

He paddled on, wondering why she had avoided answering his question about her life story. Most people jump at the chance to talk about themselves. He drew right to get the bow in a proper response attitude for the upcoming bend the eagle had vanished beyond. That's probably not in the handbook, he thought.

From its swaying perch on a bent-over cattail reed, a redwing blackbird trilled a greeting or warning. A hundred-plus-year-old spruce tree rising from the swampy soil like a green-limbed Eiffel Tower stood by, tolerating yet another passerby. At the top of the tree a crow swayed and cawed.

I like the feel of this paddle, he thought. A good old paddle, beaten and battered through the years, the summer days and hours on the river…neat, he thought. He stroked, trying to match the river's passing. How is it that so much water can flow so eternally? Why can we never seem to catch up with the water, get in the flow? He reached and reached for more and more water.

Madigan was silent, her head turning this way and that, looking here and there at the eroded banks, healthy green trees leaning over the channel, old, dry-barked, defeated trees, dead trunks sunk to their hips surrendering in death to the eternal waters flowing. "This is the most relaxed I've been in a long time. It's easy talking to you facing away like this. It's like you're not really there."

That's me, the invisible man, Davecki thought. "Nice," he said.

"I did have a time of it growing up," she said.

She slapped at her neck. She rocked the boat leaning forward to the dry bag strapped to the forward thwart. "Don't tip us over, okay?"

Ya think, he thought.

"Sounds like a plan," he said.

She pulled the Thermacell thingy from the bag, turned it on and stood it up on the hull between her blue water shoes. Settling back she said, "Mom and Dad O'Grady got me out of that business in Gurley. I went to school at Lake Superior College and St. Scholastica. Things got rough again for a while in Denver, but when the booze went away the drama and toxic marriage went with it.

"Congratulations. How'd you manage to get sober?" Davecki asked.

"I found the Lord and AA," Mercy said.

"Switching," Davecki said.

He swung the paddle over her head. Drips fell.

"Hey! You're getting me wet," Mercy said.

"It would be dryer up front."

"But then I wouldn't feel like a royal queen."

Or a royal pain, he chuckled indwardly. He reached out a sweep stroke, got the nose around, then feathered the paddle's pan in against the side of the canoe without clunking. "Look," he said.

"What?"

"Up ahead," he chin nodded.

"Where?"

"On the right, beyond the balsam." Davecki ruddered with the old paddle pointing the bow directly at the whitetail doe, its front legs in water's edge, watching them, tall ears forward, shining brown eyes unblinking.

"Oh my," Madigan said.

At her words, the doe reared back, pivoted on slender hind legs and plunged away into the brush. Her departure revealed a spotted fawn. The youngster gawked, blinked, shook its floppy ears, and then too jumped like a loaded spring, releasing its flight response in pursuit of mom and safety and solitude.

"That's a good sign. Deer are so gentle," she said.

You haven't seen them fighting each other over corn in February, he thought. He watched her shoulders rise and fall like she was gathering courage to speak.

"Like Owen said, I should have come back sooner. My shrink encouraged me for years to come back. He calls it reconciling basic youth conflicts."

"Umm," Davecki said.

"This has been good for me and for mom and dad O'Grady, particularly mom."

"I see," Davecki said. I really don't, he thought.

Madigan went silent again. The oxbows came and went. A rare fast current in the Meadow's Section sped up around a corner pushing the aluminum against the far bank. The fingers of alder and buckthorn brush scraped along the scarred hull like fingers on a chalkboard. Madigan pushed off with outstretched fingers and, leaning forward, grabbed at the grass strands, helping pull the boat along.

"Seems like your mom runs the show," Davecki said.

"For the most part," Madigan said. "But Ollie can and does put his foot down now and then."

"There's a tick on your shoulder," Davecki said.

"Get it," she yelped.

He leaned forward to pinch it off her reddening skin before it could hide in the folds of her shirt. He tossed the not quite decommissioned bio-weapon to the water, watching it churn tiny legs on the glassy surface. Sorry, tick, he thought. "Musta got on board when we bumped that grassy bank."

"Yup."

More silent gliding on peaceful waters until...Madigan coughed and shook her head and said, "I've never told anybody this, but I've read that telling secrets to strangers on...like on airplanes, is best because they don't have to do anything with the knowledge, and you never see them again."

The only thing this canoe has in common with an airplane is the aluminum, he thought. Following Anne Lamott's advice, all he said was, "Huh." He shipped paddle across his knees and let the river take the canoe and conversation where it would.

"And you're stranger than most," she laughed. It sounded like a robin's chirr, rising in volume.

"Thank you, thank you very much," Davecki trotted out Elvis again.

More silence.

She's reconsidering, Davecki thought. Miraculously, he didn't speak.

"I had the baby in Gurley."

"Really? Huh."

"I told everyone I miscarried."

Drips off the silent paddle made circles in the slow, calm water.

"The nuns just took him. I didn't even give him up for adoption."

"That had to be hard."

Madigan reached her left hand over the gunwale. She grabbed at water. Water threaded through flickering fingers. "It was and it wasn't; I was pretty messed up at the time. It got harder later."

Ahead an overhanging cedar tipped into the river like a bowing butler. The upriver branches of the cedar rose and fell into and out of the flowing current like an oilfield pump rising and falling—rising and falling restlessly.

Too late Davecki took to paddle to avoid the collision. The high nose of the canoe nudged into sopping heavy boughs that grabbed at the prow like a drowning person.

"Yikes!" Madigan yelped, fending off wet branches.

Backpaddling the relentless current, he fought the tree and the tree won. He raised paddle and backstroked at the thick branches as Madigan ducked. Cedar bobbed and weaved like Mohammad Ali throwing punches at George Foreman in the Rumble in the Jungle. Meanwhile, the much experienced Old Canoe rope-a-doped the cedar who was furiously fighting to swamp the royalty bearing barge.

Queen Madigan slunk low in the hull.

Slave Dave leaned back against the stern deck.

Old Canoe's flanks wheezed like a Covid patient against Cedar's clutching branches. River Current contributed to the fracas pushing the stern around as the bow slid away from the tree's grasping. Old Canoe executed an elegant backwards pirouette freeing itself from Cedar's clutches.

Swiping cedar shards from her arms and bust, Madigan resumed the royal repose. She looked back at Cedar shaking its green fists at the escapees. "That was fun," she said. "Your paddling skills leave a lot to be desired."

"Thanks," Davecki said. He looked over his shoulder, paddling in reverse.

"This is kinda neat," Madigan said. "Backwards down the river to grandmother's house we go."

The O'Grady's are way upriver, Davecki thought as he back-paddled toward shore. The stern bumped the river's soft underbelly. The bow swung. He stroked forward and entered the flow properly. "Sorry about that," he said.

"Why apologize? It was fun."

"You ever try to find the baby?" Davecki asked.

"No. At the time. I had a gig cleaning for the nuns at Saint Dolores. Sister Arenosa was in love with the priest. They quit the church, took off and got married in Mexico." She sighed. After a long pause she added, "With the baby." Another sigh.

"Ummm," Davecki said. He paddled onward.

"I should have kept him."

"You were messed up. Teddy Roosevelt said, 'Do the best you can with what you have where you are'," Davecki said.

"You sound like Oliver."

"That's a compliment, I take it."

"Yeah. I guess," Mercy said.

Onward Christian paddlers, paddling off to not war, Davecki thought. And so he did until around the bend came Pine Tree Landing.

"Hello!" Owen called from shore. "It's about time! Where'd you pick up the law?"

9

"Thanks for sharing, glutton," Hermit said, picking up the Unkind bar wrapper, sticking the cellophane in the back pocket of his wool pants.

Eleanor clacked her teeth showing white enamel and sticky caramel, expressing glee or disregard or both.

Hermit swung into Davecki's vest with one arm and had mucho problemo getting the other arm in. "Too small," he said, dragging the vest off. He unzipped the slash pocket. "Whoa. This is trouble," Hermit said, freeing Davecki's phone.

Eleanor pried her eyes away from her search in the dead leaves and green grass shoots for the bits and remains of the Unkind bar that she had annihilated.

Hermit took off at a trot without a word.

Eleanor looked at his departure. She sniffed the ground and lipped up an errant peanut from the Unkind bar. She looked at the engulfing brush where Hermit had gone. She shook her head and loped after.

"You and I will be putting the Grumman up," Owen O'Grady said. "If other people are involved, paint jobs get ruined."

"Oh, grow up, Owen," Mercy said. "It's just a scratch."

Owen grabbed the bow. Davecki grabbed the stern. They humped the canoe up Pine Tree Landing toward the parking lot as Mercy hoisted the paddle, PFD, Thermacell thingy, and dry bag.

"It went all the way through to the primer, Sis," Owen called over his shoulder. "Going to take a claim to get it fixed."

Unlike the father and mother, these kids believe in insurance, Davecki thought.

Canoe secure, gear stored, Mercy said, "I'll sit in back so Owen can give you the grand tour." She squeezed under the loading strap going through the cabin and fell back to her seat.

Davecki got in as the Tesla's screen came to life.

Out on the blacktop, Owen slapped the foot feed down, plastering Davecki's head back to the headrest. "Wow, lotta punch," he said.

"Tri-motor has eleven-hundred horsepower," Owen said.

"Hard to believe," Davecki said. Stanski could hurt himself with a squad like this.

Owen slowed down from 100-miles-per-hour when the Tesla seemed to want to launch off one of the road's many convolutions and undulations through the Brule State Forest.

This thing would absolutely launch going over Tickle Belly, Davecki mused.

"County ever going to fix this road?" Owen asked.

"The County likes it rough," Davecki said, "it keeps speeders like you from killing their passengers and unwary locals on their tractors, to say nothing of the abundant wildlife."

"Amen to that," came from the back seat.

O'Grady touched the gear-stalk, putting the Tesla in autopilot as a giant green gravel truck came at them. He took his hands off the steering wheel and fluttered his fingers in the air.

Davecki made to grab the wheel.

Owen swatted the grab away, laughing as Gigantor Truck rushed toward them.

"Quit being so mean, Owen," Mercy scolded.

Yeah, Owen, Davecki thought, beads of sweat erupting on his temples.

The huge green truck careened past.

Owen took control of the wheel again.

"Man," Davecki said. "That was intense."

"Takes some getting used to," Owen said. Settling down to a reasonable speed, he asked, "So, seriously, sis, how did you manage to pick up a deputy on a solo canoe outing?"

"I caught him skinny dipping in the river and made a citizen's arrest." Lilting laughter from the back seat.

"Seriously?"

"Not really," Davecki said.

"Oh?" Mercy said.

"Well, sort of. At least I had my skivvies on by the time she came along," Davecki shook his head.

"You cray-cray? Skinny dipping in the Brule this time of year? That's gotta be freezing man."

Davecki glanced at Owen. "Well, the motivation was high. I sat in a nest of wood ticks and was covered so I ran down to the river, stripped and jumped in to try and wash away the ones I couldn't see."

"Ugh," Owen said. "That makes my skin crawl."

"I came along and picked some off him," Mercy said.

"I lost count somewhere north of two hundred fifty ticks," Davecki said.

"Gives me goose bumps," Owen said, shaking his head like Misty of Chincoteague.

Silence menaced the moment until Davecki fought back, saying; "Dang! Forgot my vest up on the ridge. I'll have to go back and get it."

"It'll be crawling with ticks, I suppose," Mercy said.

"Dryer treatment," Davecki said.

"Won't that mess up your dryer?" Owen asked.

"They get caught in the lint screen for the most part," Davecki said.

"That's so gross," Mercy said.

"At least they're dead. You can pick them off the screen pretty easy," Davecki explained, pointing his face toward the window, hiding his grin.

"You've been down this road before then," Owen said.

"Not this bad. But ticks are a way of life in the spring and summer around here."

Mercy said, "Another good reason to stay away."

"Humpf," Owen humpfed. He bumped the steering wheel.

Just like Stanski, Davecki thought.

Owen said, "No ticks in winter. You could have come back for Christmas."

The pain is never far from the surface, Davecki thought.

"I thought about it many times. But I wasn't ready."

Here we go, Davecki thought.

Owen glanced at Davecki, "She's selfish."

"Taking care of mental health isn't selfish, Owen."

Owen looked at Davecki. "Here comes the lecture."

"Oh, shut up," Mercy said.

Or, don't, Davecki thought.

Again the menace of silence.

As the Tesla navigated the undulating blacktop sorely in need of repair, Davecki inclined his head toward the rear and asked, "What lecture?"

"Doggone it!" Owen said.

"You be quiet, Owen," Mercy said. "The O'Grady line hasn't been blessed with organic schizophrenia."

Owen said nothing.

"What's organic schizophrenia?" Davecki asked.

Mercy leaned forward and hung her hands on the loading strap threaded behind the headrests. "The Madigan's trace their lineage back to Roscommon in Ireland. There's been loads of studies done there on hereditary schizophrenia. In the old days in Ireland the family name was actually just Egan. But because there was a lot of schizophrenia in the family, all the Irish neighbors called them the Mad Egans. When great-grandpa emigrated during the famine he swore he told the ship's purser that his name was Egan. Grandpa said that the purser must have been a Roscommon man who wrote down Mad Egan. He figures the immigration clerk in New Orleans wrote down Madigan when he got off the coffin ship. That's what Mom O'Grady says Grandpa said."

Owen broke his silence, "What she's saying is that the Madigan's are all bat-shit crazy."

"You're talking about your mother, loser," Mercy said.

And yourself, Davecki thought.

Silence again tried to gain the upper hand.

Davecki slapped silence silly saying, "Mark Twain said, 'When we remember we are all mad, the mysteries disappear and life stands explained.'"

"You're just full of quotes, aren't you?" Mercy said.

As Owen steered the Tesla into the O'Grady turn-around, Davecki said, "Would you look at that."

"What?" Owen and Mercy asked simultaneously.

"On the mirror of my truck," Davecki said.

Owen, unFinnlander-like, and, having never read the handbook, drove the Tesla between the restored Bronco and Davecki's F-150. He asked, "That your vest?"

"Yup."

Owen touched the screen. The electronic marvel of modern transportation shut down.

Mercy's voice echoed from the rear, "I wonder if Oliver found it for you?"

"They're at the doctor's," Owen said.

"Hermit of the Brule," Davecki said.

"That piker gets around, doesn't he," Owen snarked.

10

Davecki poked at the silver dollar-sized discs of venison backstrap sizzling in the bottom of the black cast iron pan using the stainless steel slotted spoon he bought at Turner & Page's Speed Shop auction when Tuner Turner won the lottery and moved to Utah to break two world land speed records at the Bonneville Salt Flats on a snowmobile and an ATV.

"Could you hurry it up a little? I'm starving," Stanski said from the dining room table, where he read the latest copy of *The North Coast Weekly Bugle.*

"You want a good breakfast or a fast one? Corn flakes in the cupboard if you want," Davecki said, squeezing sour cream from the tube over the searing steak. He lowered the propane flame. He sprinkled on garlic salt. He smeared everything together. He scooped flat noodles from the boiling water in the pot on the back burner. He lipped a noodle to his mouth. Al dente, perfect, he thought. He shut the pot burner down. He dumped the noodles in the strainer waiting in the sink. He sprayed cold water on them. He shook the strainer.

"There's a picture here of a guy from Chicago and his trophy hundred-and-sixty-pound bear," Stanski said.

"That's so gross on so many levels," Davecki said.

"What's your problem?" Stanski asked.

Davecki stirred, said, "Well, a hundred-sixty-pound bear is hardly a trophy and why shoot a defenseless bear?"

"Umm, Dave?"

"Yeah?"

"You're cooking venison," Stanski said.

"So? At least when you put the bam in Bambi we eat the meat. Trophy bear meat mostly ends up wasted after the photo is taken and the hide is skun."

"Life as we know it," Stanski said.

"Too bad," Davecki said, dumping a can of mushroom pieces

and stems into the cast iron skillet. He stirred them in. He shook more garlic salt across the bubbling surface. He dumped noodles from the strainer to the skillet and stirred. "So, what's the stakeout plan, Stan the man?"

"Would you knock it off with the rhyming?"

"You don't like my timing?"

"My sense of humor is declining."

"More puns I'm designing."

"My irritation is climbing."

"Quit your whining."

Stanski harrumphed, "Okay. You win." He folded the newspaper and tossed it toward the trash can in the corner. It fluttered and fell on the floor, missing the basket by a foot and a half. He huffed and went to put the paper in its proper place. "All set for tomorrow morning. It will get me off patrol for a change."

Davecki lifted the cast iron skillet he bought for a dollar at Louise Lecithin's rummage sale. He carried the skillet to the table. Stanski pushed the paper down into the trash some more and returned to the table. Davecki set the skillet down on the State of Alaska trivet he bought for fifty-cents at Craig Jeffery's moving sale when Jeffery decided to circumnavigate Australia on his Triumph Bonneville with Ewan McGregor and Charley Boorman. Davecki scooped stroganoff to his plate.

"You're a real cretin, you know? You're supposed to serve guests first," Stanski said.

"Suffer, brother. Suffer." Davecki said.

Stanski reached for the red handled spoon Davecki bought for a quarter at Kenyon Jonestone's rummage sale when he decided to sell all his cows and start an internet café in Helsinki in partnership with a Finnish baker-woman named Astrid that he met online.

Stanski scooped. He picked up his fork to eat.

"Grace!" Davecki yelled.

Stanski froze, eyeballing his worthy opponent, fork in midair.

Davecki bowed his head. "Thank you, Lord Jesus, for this food, bless it to our bodies and please deliver Patrick from his addiction to my cooking. Amen."

"Amen," Stanski said. The stroganoff resumed its flight plan to his mouth. Around his chewing he said, "Your prayer's pretty disrespectful."

"God can handle it. He's got a sense of humor."

"I was talking about me, doofus," Stanski said.

"Oh, yeah. I forgot. You're the center of the universe and easily offended. Shove that pan over."

Stanski pushed the pan a little ways toward Davecki but not far enough.

"Jerk," Davecki said. He pushed out of his chair, leaned across the table, grabbed the pan handle and dragged the stroganoff across the table. He scooped. He ate, he chewed, he said, "Forgot the buns." He lurched out of his chair for the oven. "So," he said, "what time tomorrow?"

"Before dawn," Stanski said.

"Seriously? Why?"

"Catch him unawares," Stanski said.

"If you say so."

They ate in silence until Stanski asked, "So? Mercy Madigan saw you in your underwear?"

"She wasn't impressed."

"How you know that?"

"She said that as a nurse she'd seen worse," Davecki said.

"Perceptive lady."

"Thanks, pal."

"You're welcome," Stanski grinned at Davecki who didn't look up. "What you guys talk about?"

Davecki looked up. "She had a baby in Gurley when she was young."

"Sounds like real paddling talk," Stanski said. "Did you tell her about fishing a dead guy out of Boxcar Hole?" He pushed his plate away. "I am sufficiently serensified. Any more would be odious to my sensitive palate."

Davecki studied Stanski for a few seconds, shook his head, said, "I kept my mouth shut for once. Somehow she and the O'Grady bunch are tied in with the hermit business. I just haven't figured out how or why, yet."

Stanski asked, "What makes you say that? Seems like a stretch to me."

"Other than my amazing ability to intuit human nature?"

"Your grandiosity is showing, pal."

"I forgot my vest on the river and it mysteriously appeared hanging on the outside rearview mirror of my truck parked at the O'Grady place."

"Ollie O'Grady find it?"

"He was at a doctor's appointment," Davecki said.

"Sarah?"

"Same-same."

"Owen?"

Davecki sighed, looked at Stanski past furrowed brow, said, "I suppose he could have gotten his lazy bones out of bed, ran through bog and brush to find a vest he had no idea was there and out of sheer kindness of heart, returned it to its rightful owner before doing his good deed for the day, picking his sister and her slave paddler up to shuttle them back home."

"You're kinda cranky then," Stanski said.

"I'm still recovering from the trauma of death by ten thousand wood ticks."

"Right. Like how many? Six? Eight?"

"Close to three hundred."

"Seriously? Any stuck?"

"Not that I know of."

Stanski said, "Better get Doxycycline just in case. Those deer ticks are sometimes impossible to see."

"Yeah," Davecki said, resignation in his voice. He looked at the stroganoff pan.

"You're too fat for thirds, Dave," Stanski said.

As Stanski was leaving without helping with the dishes, Davecki went to the trash can. He extracted the newspaper, "You need to learn to recycle," Davecki said.

"Recycling's a joke. It all gets dumped on the future ski hill on Wisconsin Point," Stanski said.

"Your cynicism is showing, pal," Davecki said as he refolded the rag, "even a little bit of recycling helps."

"If you say so," Stanski said. He exited without closing the door.

"Jerk," Davecki yelled through the open door as Stanski waved and smiled over the roof of the slowest squad in the Badger State.

The next morning Stanski and his slow squad rolled up to Davecki's trailer before dawn. He entered the domicile unannounced and helped himself to corn flakes.

Davecki emerged from the rear of the habitation still in his skivvies. He went to the stove, plucked up the tea pot; went to the sink to fetch a not-pail of water.

"Get some clothes on, man. You're ruining my morning," Stanski said. "I'm surprised Mercy Madigan didn't have a heart attack seeing you like this."

"You're welcome for the nutrition," Davecki said.

"What? I need permission?" Stanski asked.

Davecki sighed. He placed the tea kettle. He started the flame. He scratched the back of his head.

"Not like you to be speechless in Hayfield County," Stanski said, "your pineal gland mishandling your circadian rhythms lately?

Davecki said nothing. He headed out of the kitchen.

"Dave no fun," Stanski said. He rattled his spoon into the bowl with Christmas trees painted around the outside circumference. He shoved the bowl aside. He picked up the cosmetic case on the table. He opened the case. He fingered out black. He looked in the mirror. He scrubbed the black cover-up across his forehead, his cheeks, and chin. "The Hermit's going down," he said. He fingered green from the case to his face.

"How do I look?" he asked Davecki when he returned fully dressed.

"Stan? Is that you? I hear your voice but can't see you," Davecki said.

"You're not funny. You know that don't you?" Stanski said.

"So I've been told."

"You want some of this?" Stanski asked. He proffered the cosmetic case.

"I don't do makeup," Davecki said. "You have a corn flake stuck on your chin."

"Your recalcitrance is going to mess up this mission," Stanski said. He fingered the escapee corn flake from his chin with his blackened digit and stuck it in his mouth.

"You know," Davecki said, "my recalcitrance may actually be a good thing on this stake out. If the Hermit spots me and avoids me, his detour may well take him right to your perfectly camouflaged self."

"Anything's possible," Stanski said, "but it would be better if you took this seriously and went full camo."

"I'm just Auxiliary," Davecki said.

"That excuse is getting old, pal."

Davecki smirked. He pushed back from the table, "Nothing to it but to do it."

"Where to fearless leader?" Stanski asked.

"Back to where he picked up my vest. I'm hoping my Hank's jerky is still there."

"Dream on," Stanski said.

They left the trailer as the very first faint hints of dawn tickled the eastern skyline with feather-duster rays of filigree light.

The light of dawn seeped through the woods, illuminating Davecki's perch halfway up the steep bank on the west side of the Brule. Honeysuckle abounded, the delicate yellow flowers making bright dots in the dim woods like tiny vibrant Christmas tree lights strung helter-skelter across the open forest floor. A few sluggish honeybees moved from yellow blossom to yellow blossom.

Davecki pulled out his phone. The screen read 4:30 a.m. Sweet, he thought, a signal. He turned on the flashlight app. He scanned the ground for a wood tick nest. Seeing none, he sat. He got comfortable. He typed: *how come i not heering music?* He poked send. He looked away from the screen across the valley. The dim outlines of hardwood and fir trees hunkered around his position. The forest for the trees sloped away downhill toward the Brule. Somewhere over there on the other hillside, Stanski hid.

The phone screen lit up: *quit texting you ruin stakeout what music.*

"Humph," he humphed. He texted back: *ever time i watch nature show on tv music playing no music here now.*

OMG SHUT UP.

Stann no funnn. Davecki typed, touched send, and put his phone in the pocket of his Carhart jacket.

At 7:15 a.m. Davecki woke up to the sound of music; not Julie Andrews, something better, the song of a red-eyed vireo singing from the top of the canopy. "Huh?" he mumbled. He looked around. Oh yeah, the stakeout, he thought. He rubbed his eyes. He stroked his chin. He pulled out his phone. Typed, *freezing heading to truck*

Davecki waited while the F-150's engine warmed. Ten minutes later, Stanski opened the truck's passenger door. He tossed his camo gloves to the foot pan. "Oh man, that heat feels good." He climbed into the truck, his camo canvas suit rustling like he was a moving pile of fall leaves.

"Yeah, I got cold up there on the ridge where the rabbits and the hermits wouldn't go, and I couldn't find my jerky," Davecki said.

"You should get your heart checked," Stanski said. "Your circulation is shot if you got cold that easy."

"Don't should on me."

"You're stealing Mercy Madigan's riff," Stanski said. He smirked. He pulled his camo stocking cap off. The knuckles of his fist hit the roof like an exploding popcorn kernel bonking the popper cover. "You have any other big ideas? This one sucks."

Davecki huffed. He corner-eyed Stanski. "We could borrow

Charlie Greener's beagle Benny and see if the Hermit leaves good scent trails."

Stanski said, "Some jerk-wad coyote hunter shot Benny last winter, said he thought a beagle was a coyote. Guy was lucky Greener didn't kill him."

"Bummer. Guess we'll have to turn to man's other best friend," Davecki said.

"And that would be?"

Davecki smirked, "Dog spelled backwards is still man's best friend."

"You need some new material," Stanski said.

"Stan no fun."

"So I've been told."

Davecki bowed his head, said, "Our Father who art in heaven, help us find the Hermit of the Brule and bring him to justice, amen."

Stanski raised his head, stared at Davecki. "Justice?"

"Yeah, you know, payment for his crimes."

Stanski huffed, "Nobody's guilty of anything anymore, Dave. If it weren't for citizen complaints, I'd be willing to leave the Hermit alone."

"A true public servant."

"So I've been told," Stanski said. "If you have a better idea, I'm all ears."

Davecki's turn to huff. "Now you're stealing Ross Perot's material? You ever have an original thought?"

"No," Stanski said.

Davecki's turn to eyeball Stanski.

"What you looking at?" Stanski asked.

"Just checking to see how you're holding up under the pressure."

"What pressure?' Stanski asked.

"The pressure of giving up control and asking for help."

"Very funny."

Davecki huffed. "I thought you said I'm not funny."

Stanski huffed back. "You're not. It's called irony."

"More like sarcasm," Davecki said.

Stanski ripped open a hook and loop cargo pocket. He produced a wet-wipe packet and proceeded to de-camouflage his face. He looked at the smudged wet-wipe. "Huh, wood tick," he said. He powered down the window. Flicked it away. "How many ticks total did you have the other day?" he asked.

"Sixty-seven in all," Davecki answered. "Must be a Guinness Record."

"You said fifty-one earlier."

"Picky. Picky," Davecki said. He put the truck in drive. He headed for home. "I'm feeling all creepy-crawly now."

"Suffer, brother, suffer."

"You wouldn't be so cavalier if you'd suffered the trauma of ten thousand ticks."

"Now it's ten thousand?"

"Poetic license," Davecki said.

11

On the road again, Stanski and Davecki suffered the presence of silence badly. Davecki smacked serenity down, saying, "Grab the steering wheel. I think I've got a tick."

Stanski leaned over. He grabbed the truck's steering wheel with his left hand.

Davecki unbuttoned his shirt. He pulled the shirttail out of his pants. He lifted his t-shirt up and nabbed a black crawling dot from his white belly.

"Little bugger," he said. He cranked the window down. He flicked the tick just as the truck ran off the road. "What in the world!" he yelled, grabbing the wheel. He jerked the wheel left. The truck slewed from the gravel shoulder back to the blacktop of Highway 97.

"Oops!" Stanski said. "I was looking to see if there really was a tick or if it was just your imagination."

"Sheesh!" Davecki said. "Some driver you are. No wonder they gave you a super slow squad."

"Lighten up, bro."

Davecki smirked. "Oh, sorry. I forgot how sensitive you are."

Stanski said nothing.

"What? No insult?"

Stanski smiled. "I'm trying to recalibrate our conversational style into a healthier emotional model."

"Those C.E. classes in the new policing are making a difference," Davecki said.

Silence again tried to sneak a small sense of serenity to the situation.

Davecki squashed the futile attempt asking, "So, what you been thinking?"

Stanski sighed, "We should probably go do some detectoring out at Hall Rapids. Maybe find that three-fifty-seven Madigan lost."

"Well, well, well, you're finally admiting my idea has merit," Davecki said.

"It takes me a while, sometimes, you know, for me to move your suggestions from stupid to nothing-to-lose."

"Your confidence in me is underwhelming."

"I try," Stanski said.

"Umm, detectoring?" Davecki asked.

"Like that show on TV."

"Never heard of it," Davecki said. "I like the sound of detectivising better." He rubbed his chin, "There's a TV show?"

"So woefully uninformed," Stanski said.

"That's healthy sounding," Davecki snarked, putting the truck in a proper response attitude between the Ioniq squad and the front stoop of his trailer.

Stanski sighed. He popped his door. It banged into the stoop's handrail.

"Hey! My paint!" Davecki said.

"If you could replace your stale sense of humor with some new material, your paint job would be safe. Just pull ahead," Stanski said. He bounced the door against the wood some more.

"Knock it off, pal," Davecki said. He let the truck roll forward. "When you thinking of detectoring?"

"I took the liberty to liberate the detector from stores. It's in the trunk."

"Waders, too?"

"Yep."

Rolling the truck away from the stoop so Stanski could get out, Davecki said, "You load the canoe, I'll get my waders, and we'll be off," Davecki said.

"You're the one who's off, way off," Stanski smirked.

"I feel so much better all of a sudden."

Stanski dragged the canoe from behind the garage, freed the Ioniq of its burdens of metal detector and waders, and waited. And waited. "What took you so long?" he asked, when Davecki finally appeared.

"Can't go detectoring on the river without sustenance," Davecki said, lifting an old Boyscout knapsack. "Snacks," he said.

They threw Davecki's Old Town Discovery into the truck along with PFDs, a shovel, the detector, and Stanski's Simms waders. At Winneboujou landing, they floated their boat alongside a bevy of kayakers and other canoeists. As they donned their waders, one of the canoeists at the landing, a middle aged man with a Hawaiian shirt covering a ponderous pot belly asked, "You need a canoe *and* waders?"

"Yep," Stanski said.

Davecki inhaled deeply.

"Seems a bit much," the man said. He swept his right hand across his longish graying hair ending in a stubby pig tail.

That belly's a bit much, Davecki didn't say. Davecki gave Stanski raised eyebrows.

Stanski knew it was up to him to give *the answer*. He stood. He hiked his waders up, turning toward Paunchy Man, displaying his badge.

The man's face slackened. He said, "Have a nice day." He returned to his group, and they made haste to hasten downriver.

"Works every time," Stanski said.

"Yep," Davecki said, getting upright and strapped into his waders.

Stanski shuffled to the boat. He pushed it over the landing's timber edge into the water and steadied it against the stout beams fronting the flow of silvery liquid gliding past. "I'm in stern," Stanski said.

"Not," Davecki said. "It's my boat. I'm driving."

"Jerk."

"Thank you. I thought you were wanting to recalibrate our conversational style for a more healthy relationship," Davecki said as he seated himself in stern.

"Double jerk," Stanski said, taking the bow seat.

Down the river and through the woods to Hall Rapids they went. The canoe knew the way to carry the fray through water both white and slow.

From the stern, "Look at that sky, Stan. Have you ever seen anything so big and bold and blue?"

Stanski reached for more water with the cracked yellow blade of the plastic paddle, executing a pull stroke. "It's nice," he said.

"Nice? It's gorgeous," Davecki said. He clunked the gunwale with the shaft of his wooden paddle as he dug his own water, feathering the stern to the right. "There's ginger snaps in the knapsack, Stan. Grab some. Your blood sugar's low."

Stanski shipped his paddle, twisted to the knapsack strapped around the thwart and rustled out some calories. He munched as Davecki piloted.

"Better?" Davecki asked.

"Nothing like ginger snaps to cheer a guy up."

"So, your sulk she is finis?" Davecki imitated Poirot.

"Yup," Stanski said as the Discovery nosed into the alders hanging low over the shallow riverside water above Hall Rapids. Stanski grabbed an alder branch. He pulled the canoe into the brush. The bow hit the mossy shore. The stern swung downriver. Stanski stepped out into the calf-deep water. He grabbed the gunwale. He heaved the nose against the brushy shore. The boat rocked.

"Easy," Davecki yelped. He tossed his paddle beside the bagged metal detector and shovel lying in the hull bottom.

Stanski grabbed the gunwale and steadied the craft.

Davecki bent forward and made to step out. When his one foot was just over the side, Stanski tipped the boat to near swamping.

"Arrrgh!" Davecki yelled as he leapt from the canoe, moving like the dancing hippo in *Fantasia.* He splashed sideways into the pool of calm backwater on the lee side of the bend in the river. "I kill you!" he imitated *Achmed the Terrorist,* managing to stay upright and dry.

"This is getting funner and funner," Stanski grinned like the Cheshire cat.

"You're not funny. You know that don't you?" Davecki said.

"So I've been told."

They both grabbed the boat and heaved it through the alders and up onto the bank so that only a foot of stern kissed the shallow water.

Stanski handed Davecki the round nosed, long handled shovel. He freed the metal detector from its bag. He donned earphones and plugged into the metal detector. They waded into the upper reaches of Hall Rapids.

Davecki leaned on his shovel handle. His weight wedged the spaded pan deeper into the river bottom. He watched Stanski sweep the rapids. With each step Stanski swung the coil assembly under the water in front of him. After every other sweep, the deputy lifted the dripping coil from the water and adjusted the angle of the head.

Davecki looked downriver. A white pine tree well over a hundred feet tall raised its platter limbs in praise to the blue sky as the wind whispered breathy secrets to the always listening monarch of the forest. At the top of the hundred and fifty year old royal tree, a blob of black akin to a Christmas ornament in a December living room. The blob unfolded and lofted into the air like a feather drifting upwards from a leaky pillow. As the bird flew closer its white head became visible, moving forth and back, studying the action below. Its white tail feathers pivoted this way and that as it carved a course upriver. Davecki followed the eagle's flight path to above the rapids where it swerved a sharp angle in the air, arcing into the azure sky, vanishing beyond the treetops. "Sweet," he mumbled, smiling.

Down the rapids, head-phoned Stanski waved a come-hither, a big grin on his face pinched narrow by the bulbous headphones. He pointed toward his feet. He waved another come-hither. He lifted the detector aside and bent low, sticking his hand underwater.

Staggering across the rocky bottom, Davecki watched as Stanski pulled up a handful of rocks that he swept across the detector's coil.

Stanski shrugged, tossed the rocks aside and reached underwater for another handful of stones. He hollered something Davecki couldn't hear above the rapids cheering like Lambeau fans after a third down conversion.

Davecki wobbled up.

Stanski pointed down at the water between them, yelled, "Dig!"

"It wouldn't be buried in two days," Davecki yelled back.

"I know. I know," Stanski yelled, "but it's a strong signal!"

Davecki plunged the shovel into the water and dug at the bottom. As he lifted the shovel's pan, the swift current swept sand and dirt away, the effluent swirling like a swishing horse's tail in the wind. The first load held rocks ranging in size from green peas to golf balls.

Stanski swept the shovel with the detector. "Nothing."

Shovelful two yielded more sand and smaller gravel.

Stanski plunged the detector under water, swept the spot again.

"Still there," Stanski yelled. "Deeper!"

Davecki dug. Shovel three was mostly sand, but, sticking out of the muddy mixture, an encrusted three-inch long jackknife with discolored green rivets holding the white remnants of a handle that flaked to the touch.

"Whoa!" Stanski yelped, picking the artifact from the shovel's pan.

"Wow!" Davecki said as Stanski twisted the knife in the sunlight filtering through the tall trees bending over the river to observe.

Buoyed by the jackknife success, Stanski managed to stagger up and down the rapids for another half hour. After the fifteenth pop-top and the twelfth old beer can the men looked at each other in amazement as the empty Old Town bounced down the rapids between them.

"Whoa!" Stanski yelled.

Like a horse with the bit in its teeth, the canoe disobeyed and ran the rapids just fine without human involvement.

Both muttering, they staggered down-rapids and caught up with the Discovery bobbing peacefully in the calm water at the next bend.

"Where's the paddles?" Stanski asked, looking at the empty bottom of the boat.

"And the PFDs!" Davecki said.

"And the bag for the detector!" Stanski yelped.

"And the snack sack," Davecki cried.

"Had to be the Hermit," Stanski said, dragging the canoe ashore.

"Right," Davecki said.

Without a word between them, they both headed back upriver where they found Owen O'Grady and Mercy Madigan de-boating in the exact spot where the Discovery had been.

"Did you guys send our canoe down the river?" Stanski asked.

Brother and sister looked at each other like old-timers trying to understand the Internet. "No," O'Grady said. "We just got here. We're going to try and find Mercy's Colt." He lifted a metal detector from the hull of the red Grumman.

Great minds think alike, Davecki thought.

"Somebody did," Stanski said, anger tinting his comment.

"We just got here," Mercy said. She held her paddle across her body like a cudgel stick. "Look!" she said, gesturing with paddle tip toward the fastest section of water going past.

They turned to see a paddle shooting down the fuzzy water going north. Moments later paddle number two went past, bouncing down the rapids.

"He's toying with us," Stanski said.

"Who?" Owen asked.

"The Hermit," Stanski growled.

"Or Winneboujou," Davecki grinned.

"Who's Winneboujou?" Mercy asked.

"Don't get him started," Stanski said.

"Look," Owen said, pointing at the river.

The metal detector's black shroud of not-Turin swept by on the current looking like an undulating blanket.

"Well, at least he returned that," Stanski said.

"But not the cookies," Davecki mourned.

"What are you two doing here?" Owen asked.

"Same as you," Davecki said, "looking for the lost shaker of salt."

"Not funny," Mercy said.

PFDs ran the rapids next.

"You're really looking for the gun?" Owen said.

"Great minds think alike," Stanski said.

"We should get our stuff," Davecki said.

"Who's Winneboujou?" Mercy asked.

"He's the Anishinaabe Trickster who likes to pull stunts on hapless humans," Davecki said.

"He can tell you more some other time," Stanski said. "Right now we've got gear to catch up with." He started downriver with a, "Good luck!" over his shoulder.

"Let us know if you find the gun," Davecki said, splashing after the departing Stanski.

Madigan and O'Grady watched a bit, shrugged their shoulders and commenced to unloading their canoe.

Upriver fifty yards, from under the canopy of drooping and concealing balsam limbs, Hermit and Eleanor watched, big grins on both faces.

In the Ioniq shuttling back to the truck, Davecki said, "We covered it pretty good. I don't think they'll find it."

"I'd say the chances of *anyone* finding it are slim to none, and Slim left town," Stanski said.

"Them coming out like that lends credibility to her story," Davecki said.

"Yep," Stanski said.

"The good news is," Davecki said, "we now know the Hermit wants to play."

Stanski huffed. "Granted," he said, "only thing is, playtime's over."

"There's that," Davecki said, "but there's something else more important."

"Oh? What? Did I miss some clue?"

"No. Can't this thing go any faster? I'm starving," Davecki complained.

Stanski patted his right leg: "It's to the metal, pal."

12

Oliver O'Grady leaned into the handle of the yellow DeFault impact driver with sufficient force to drive the three-inch deck screw deep into the thick bark of Grandfather Pine. Pulling the trigger on the pistol-like tool, the screw twisted through the tree's three-inch skin, reaching sapwood. If this was Narnia, the tree would have complained. Even still, Ollie wouldn't have heard, busy as he was putting the Cuddeback bear box in alignment with the more-or-less clear area in the shelter of Grandfather's arms.

"That should do it," O'Grady said, patting the box containing the camera that was going to capture the thief of the Brule dead to rights. Next he went to the young Ironwood tree holding the sawed-off L.C. Smith double barrel level. He tightened the black zip-ties securing the trip-gun to the tree trunk. "Good enough for who it's for," he muttered. He picked up the monofilament line wrapped around one of the triggers. He unraveled the spool, strung it behind the tent stake driven into the ground behind and below the gun. He backed away from the stake, playing out the trip wire as he retreated toward Grandfather Pine, holder of the camera.

O'Grady's L.L. Jean boot heel caught accidentally on an exposed pine tree root. Or maybe Grandfather Pine intentionally tripped the salty old feller. Twisting to avoid falling and breaking a hip, he jerked on the tripwire, the gun fired, and Oliver O'Grady had more than a broken hip to worry about.

"**O**ld fool," Hermit said, rushing out from the tag alders. He ran past the gun still pulsing white smoke wafting from one of the barrels, Eleanor hot on his heels.

O'Grady was flat on his back on the ground, eyes rolled back into his head, his face, speckled with flecks of white and spots of red, Hermit put two fingers to the old man's wattled neck. "Not dead, El," he reported. El licked at the drops of red oozing from the old man's face that looked like he had the measles. Hermit licked his finger. He swept it across a particularly white patch on Oliver's messed up face and tasted. Hermit turned to Eleanor standing with two front paws on the old man's shoulder. "Rock salt, El. He'll be okay."

"Hissa-hiss," Eleanor said.

O'Grady groaned.

"I know. I know. He'll have a hard time explaining it, but that's not our problem." Hermit went to the trip gun. He pulled his Leatherman PST II tool and cut the zip ties. He clipped the monofilament off. He took the gun to the bear box. Not unlike a big black bear, he hammered on the box with the butt of the shotgun until the box popped open. He took the camera apart, extracted the SD card, and headed for the hills.

"These don't look like allergic reactions," Sarah O'Grady said as she daubed calamine lotion on Ollie's face. "More like little craters."

O'Grady, seated in the straight-backed chair next to the dining room table with the still unfinished puzzle, said, "All I know is I tripped and fell face first into a nettle plant; I wish you'd use the DMSO. It works better than calamine."

"No way, mister, that stuff's just turpentine," the Mrs. said.

"Is not. It's a miracle cure," the suffering patient said.

"What were you doing out there anyway?" Mrs. O'Grady asked. "How did you get so wet? She lifted her soggy arm from her husband's shoulder and dried her forearm off on her own Stormy Kromer shirt.

"I was putting the trail camera out to see if I could get a pic of the hermit."

"They tried that three years ago, Ollie. Did you forget?"

"No, I did not forget. Don't go building a case for putting me in a memory care unit."

Sarah shook her head and rolled her eyes. "Why so wet?"

"I went right away to the river and drenched myself," he said. "To wash away the nettle juice," he lied again.

Looking doubtful, Sarah said, "I see." She daubed more calamine.

"No you don't."

"You don't have to be so grouchy, old man," Sarah said.

"Sorry, my queen. I apologize."

"That's better. You should have brought the nettle plant back. We could make nettle tea. It's supposed to be good for your prostate."

Oliver put his arm around Sarah's waist, pulling her close. "Not as good as getting eggs from Harry' hens. He was right about eating eggs from chickens where the rooster runs free." Grinning, he said, "I know what would be good for my prostate just now."

Smiling herself, Queen Sarah set the calamine lotion aside. "Your inner rooster is showing," she said, straddling his lap.

"Thank you, Lord, for high-T eggs," Oliver said.

"Amen and amen," Sarah said undoing shirt buttons.

Stanski steered the Ioniq to within half a foot of the trailer's stoop.

Davecki opened his door and clunked it repeatedly against the wooden steps. "You know your sense of humor could use an upgrade, don't you? This joke is getting old."

"What's good for the goose is good for the gander," Stanski said. He looked past Davecki to the porch stoop. "What the heck is that?"

Davecki looked where Stanski stared.

A battered old shotgun lay against the screen door. Stanksi put the car in drive, letting it roll forward. They got out. Davecki picked up the gun, opened the breach, sniffed the chamber. "Recently fired." He handed it to Stanski.

Stanski twisted the weapon around, examining it. "He strike you as a guy who'd do this to his firearm?" He handed the Smith back to Davecki pointing to the underside of the fore stock.

Davecki held the gun while studying the stock, pondering the O'GRADY scratched deeply into the dark finish as if with a dull nail. "Not at all. He was pretty anal about his firewood pile."

"What the heck is it doing here?" Stanski said.

"Ten bucks it's the Hermit's work," Davecki said.

"Ya think?" Stanski said.

"You've got some 'splainin' to do, Ollie," Davecki said.

"It's not my gun," Oliver O'Grady answered Stanski's question as they gathered on the screen porch.

"Really?" Sarah O'Grady said. "I thought you had one something like it only longer."

Davecki raised an eyebrow at Stanski.

Stanski shook his head no, issuing an imperceptible gag order.

"No, my double is a Damascus barrel ten gauge." He handed the open-breached gun back to Davecki.

I'd like a good look at your gun cabinet, Davecki didn't say. Bet there's a gap where this recently stood, he thought. He asked, "So why is your name scratched into the stock?" Davecki turned the fore stock toward O'Grady brandishing the crudely carved brand at the old man.

"I'm thinking it's the Hermit trying to incriminate me," O'Grady said.

"Why on earth would he do that?" Sarah asked.

"To take the heat off him," Oliver answered.

"I suppose," Stanski said, sounding unconvinced.

"Blame the victim is a classic move," Davecki said, sounding unconvinced.

"Why would the Hermit dislike you?" Stanski asked.

"Maybe I don't replace my grill's propane tank fast enough for him."

"Speaking of which," Sarah said, "when are you going to do that?"

"I was going to do it earlier, but fell into that nettle plant," O'Grady said.

Don't look like stings, Davecki thought.

"Plus, some people keep distracting me," Ollie said, a glint in his eyes.

Sarah smirked, said, "Well, that explains it." She looked at the floor.

Something's happening here, Davecki thought. What it is ain't exactly clear.

"Well, as it's not your gun and it was left on Dave's stoop, we'll keep it as evidence. Maybe someone will report it stolen. In the meantime keep your doors locked," Stanski said.

"My Ruger is loaded," O'Grady said.

"Don't, honey," Sarah said.

Yeah honey, don't, Davecki thought.

"Don't go making a huge mistake, Mr. O'Grady," Stanski said.

"I'm just standing my ground," O'Grady said, his eyes fierce now.

Seems pretty fired up, Davecki thought, too much caffeine today?

Stanski said, "Things are changing in that regard."

"Not in Wisconsin," O'Grady said.

"Just be careful. Lotta people get shot with their own weapons," Stanski said.

"I'm not a lot of people."

"Oh, Ollie! I wish you wouldn't be so hostile," Sarah said.

"Just protecting my queen," Oliver O'Grady said.

His queen blushed.

"Well, thanks for your time," Stanski said.

In the Ioniq, Stanski said, "That was sort of weird."

"Yeah, something's going on between them," Davecki said.

"He's lying about the shotgun," Stanski said.

"Ya think?" Davecki quipped. He scratched the back of his neck. He produced yet another wood tick. Pinching the bug, powering down the window, and flicking the carcass away, he said, "You'd think some scientist would come up with a way to eradicate wood ticks entirely.

"Seems like he's itching for a fight," Stanski said.

Davecki powered the window back up. "You're not listening to me again."

"If you'd say something worth hearing, I'd listen," Stanski said.

Davecki returned to the case at hand. "I just hope O'Grady doesn't gun the Hermit down in cold blood."

Stanski drummed the steering wheel.

"What?" Davecki asked.

Stanski did not look away from his driving.

"Come on, hoser, what's in that peak-ed little brain of yours?"

Stanski, without looking, said, "Shouldn't it be gunned down in warm blood? I mean, if it was cold blood, the vic would already be dead and it wouldn't be murder she wrote."

Davecki smiled. "I've got to hand it to you, Stan. You've managed to ruin a good metaphor. Nice work, man."

"Be that as it may, IF," Stanski made the if big, "Ollie shoots the Hermit in cold or warm blood, he'll have way more trouble than a simple B&E to deal with."

"IF he does, he'll drag the body inside and claim self defense," Davecki said.

"Yep." Stanski sighed.

Davecki rubbed his chin.

Stanski sighed-sighed again, "What?"

"Whatta-ya mean, what?"

Stanski said, "Whenever you rub your chin like that you're thinking something important."

"I'm thinking French toast."

"French toast for supper. I like it," Stanski said. He slammed his foot to the floor. The Ioniq shuddered a little at the abuse. "Pathetic," Stanski said.

14

At the trailer door, Davecki bent to the stoop. "What have we here?" He picked up an SD card resting on the handrail.

"It's an SD card," Stanski said.

"Captain Obvious," Davecki said. He looked around the driveway, looked toward the sauna, looked back to the blacktop at the end of the drive. "It's irritating," he said, opening the door.

Stanski followed, asked, "What's irritating?"

"The Hermit," Davecki said, plinking the SD card down on the counter. "He comes and goes as he pleases, trespassing at will whenever and wherever he wants. Next thing I know he'll be taking sauna without my permission."

"I don't think hermits are in to sauna-ing," Stanski said. "Where's your laptop?"

"He must have left it at the same time he dropped the shotgun off," Davecki said.

"And we didn't notice it?" Stanski said.

"How come in all the hermit research I've been doing, there's not one mention of how bad a hermit must smell? Laptop's in the back bedroom." Davecki opened the fridge, pulling components.

Stanski returned with the laptop as Davecki turned components into nutrition.

"This is something else," Stanski said from the kitchen table.

"What?" Davecki asked as he added another slice of steaming French toast to the stack of plates on the counter next to the stove.

"The video shows Ollie O'Grady setting up a trip-gun and getting blasted by the shotgun he doesn't remember owning."

Davecki plunked the plates and pile of French toast on the table. He walked around the table to view the laptop screen. There in full color evidence, complete with time and date stamp, the unsuitable for work scene of Ollie tripping, getting blasted with a white powder, the Hermit zipping in, a raccoon scampering, Hermit tending to Ollie, dismantling the trip gun, and then what seemed like an earthquake, all played out in graphic detail.

"Huh," Davecki said. He went to the fridge. He retrieved more components with a detour to the silverware drawer.

They got their priorities straight. They sat, said grace, commenced to partake of French toast in the evening.

"Now what?" Davecki asked, pouring maple syrup from a pint jar.

"We arrest Oliver O'Grady," Stanski said, buttering.

"On what charge? Shooting himself with rock salt?" Davecki leaned forward. He stabbed the plate holding the last two slices of French toast and dragged it across the table.

"Hey!" Stanski said, "I was going to take one of those."

"You snooze, you lose," Davecki said.

Stanski said, "He lied to us."

"So? Lying to the police is a national pastime," Davecki said.

"True, but…still, spring guns are illegal."

"Let it go, Stan."

"Don't wanna," Stanski said.

"Well then, you go out there, cuff him, charge him, and show up in court when Judge Ledeen fines him and sends him home with a reprimand," Davecki said.

"You're no fun."

"It's like that guy out east who stole all those antique rifles and got one day in jail for it because he was eighty. These days you do the crime you don't do the time," Davecki said. He picked up plates, went to the sink, said, "The better plan is to trap the Hermit with Cheetos."

"What?"

"You heard me. The Hermit is always taking food. I say we bait him like a bear."

"And what we going to do when he takes the bait? Shoot him and send a trophy pic to the Bugle?"

"We tackle him. We cuff him. We put him in jail and charge him…"

"…with what?" Stanski interrupted. "Living off the land?"

"...unlawful camping," Davecki continued.

"Going to have to look that statute up," Stanski said, moving to the sink.

"We'd be heroes," Davecki said as he washed dishes.

Stanski, drying a plate, said, "Ledeen will slap his wrist and send him on his way. Back to the boonies to continue in his sorta-life of sorta-crime."

"True. I hear the recidivism rate for hermits is ninety-eight percent," Davecki said. "But he will be out of the burglary business."

"And why's that?"

"His hideout will be destroyed by the DNR. Ledeen will put a bracelet on him. If he misses one meeting with Probation and Parole, he'll be treated to an all-expenses-paid long- term visit to another part of the Brule River State Forest where eighty-nine other hooligans are housed. The thought of ten to fifteen inside the Gordon Prison will be a significant deterrent. He'll straighten out and fly right," Davecki said.

"You're probably right. Why Cheetoes," Stanski asked.

"He stole their Cheez-its didn't he? Toss in some cookies and a one pound propane tank as aperitif it will be like honey to a bear."

Stanski put a plate in the countertop, "You could bake your oatmeal raisin cookies for him."

"I'm not making cookies for the Hermit."

"We could garnish it with some smoked fish from Sophie's," Stanski said.

"No way," Davecki said, "that stuff's too good for the Hermit."

15

The six-foot-tall glossy buckthorn at the side of the yard was unmoved by the "Caw-caw-caw" of the black crow in the blue sky above. "Roger that Elvis," the Hermit of the Brule said as the buckthorn moved like Birnam Wood. The black dot in the blue sky caw-cawed in response. Across the lawn he walked, followed by Eleanor, scooting alongside. At the white storm door at the back of the cabin with false red shutters not protecting the windows, Hermit tried the latch. The screen door opened, but the knob on the main door did not turn. "Some people's children, Eleanor, they just gotta make life difficult," he said.

"Chitter-chit," Eleanor answered. She put both front paws on the wooden door and bounced like a polar bear pounding ice, to no effect.

"Thanks for the help, little one, but more effective methods are in order." Hermit pulled the butter knife from his Captain Kangaroo pocket. He poked the knife's blunt point between the door stop and the jamb. White paint chips popped off the jamb as Hermit pushed the knife through. He pumped the knife handle down and up like getting water from a well. The knife slid forth and back as he twisted the doorknob and jiggled the loose door in its frame. "Lord help us," he prayed. When the knife jumped and the door opened, Hermit said, "The Lord helps those who pray, El."

Eleanor chittered and ran inside.

The burglar shuffled across the cabin's main room to a row of cupboards hanging from the wall to the left of the '40s era Coolerator, whose enamel door stood open showing bare wire shelving. He opened a cupboard door above the sink. He pulled a plastic Super One Foods bag from the other Captain Kangaroo pocket and downloaded canned goods to the bag. He pulled down a cellophane packet of snickerdoodle cookies. He opened a drawer below the countertop. He pulled out a sharp knife and sliced the packet open. "Umm," he said. He put the cookies into the sack.

Eleanor tugged on his pants leg. "Chit-chit-chit."

"You're on a diet, remember?" Hermit said.

Eleanor hissed and jumped on his lower leg, clinging with all four paws.

Hermit crossed the open room in a limp with Eleanor holding on like a huge furry tumor.

At a shelf loaded with books beside the window opposite the kitchen area, he bent and studied the titles.

Eleanor de-tumored and returned to the kitchen in search of crumbs.

Hermit pulled *The Way West*. It went in the bag. *The Partner* followed.

He moved to a small table under the window where soft sunlight through dusty lace curtains illuminated a blood pressure wrist cuff and pill bottles. Reaching for the baby aspirin he froze in mid-gesture at the, "DON'T MOVE A MUSCLE, OR I'LL SHOOT," that sounded behind him.

"Keep your hands where I can see them. Down on the floor, now," the voice commanded.

Hermit raised his free hand to the ceiling and lifted his bag hand a little higher. He started to turn toward the voice.

"Don't turn around, just get down...NOW!"

Hermit made to kneel at the same moment the voice yelled, "WHAT IN THE!" followed by the sound of twenty toenail claws skittering across linoleum flooring, followed by the voice yelling, "GET AWAY!"

Hermit took off for the back door, grinning to see Eleanor lunging at the man with no gun, her bare teeth exposed and throat hissing hatred.

The screen door slapped as Hermit bolted, goodie bag still in hand. He sprinted across the lawn toward the thorn-less glossy buckthorn. He looked up at Crow circling and yelled, "Thanks a lot, Elvis!" The screen door slapped again as Eleanor fled at high speed. It slapped a third time followed by the man yelling, "Don't ever come back unless you want to get shot!"

Hermit ran through the briars and he ran through the brambles. He ran through thickets where only Eleanor dared to go. At river's edge, he stopped. Panting like a hound dog, he leaned against a thick trunked cedar. Eleanor scampered up. She put her paws on Hermit's right leg and started climbing. Hermit reached down. He grabbed Eleanor by the scruff of the neck and cradled her under one arm.

"Chitter-chit!" Eleanor scolded.

"I'm sorry. I'm sorry. I was as surprised as you. Elvis said the place was empty."

Eleanor bared teeth in a smile or a threat.

"Don't get your underwear in a bundle. No harm, no foul," Hermit said.

Eleanor wiggled her nose. She blinked her black eyes in the middle of her masked face. She licked her black lips.

Breathing settling some, Hermit sat on the thick trunk of a downed cedar that had grown after falling and was now a gentle fifty-foot-long C-curve arching upward toward the sun.

"Huh," he said. He patted Eleanor's head. "See? Putting you on a diet is a good thing. You get crabby and irritable and eager to take out your subliminated hostility on innocent bystanders. Good girl!" he said.

Eleanor laid her snout on his lap and raised her eyes like an inquisitive Labrador.

"Okay. Okay," Hermit sighed, shaking his head. He pulled the snickerdoodles from the sack.

Eleanor sat up and took the cookie in her teeth from Hermit's extended fingers.

"I'm tempted to say, Body of Christ," Hermit said.

Eleanor put both paws to the cookie, snapping it in half.

Hermit partook of his own communion and muttered, "Mmm."

Masticating the tasty treat he picked up the Grisham. He fanned pages. Swallowing snickerdoodle he read out loud, "They found him in Ponta Pora, a pleasant little town in Brazil, on the border of Paraguay, in a land still known as the Frontier."

"Chitter, chitter, chit, chit," Eleanor said, shards of cookie spewing from the sides of her her pointy jaw.

"I agree. Nice first line."

Hermit continued reading to himself. El stuck her nose toward the cookies.

"No, you don't," Hermit said. He put his hand over the snickerdoodles. "Your diet, remember?"

Eleanor raised up on her heavy haunches. She waved her hands at him, hissing.

"I know. I know. I'm ungrateful." He pulled another cookie, "Just one more as your reward for helping out back there."

Eleanor took the cookie. She looked at Hermit, shook her head, and waddled to the end of the lower end of the chaise lounge cedar where she and ate in sullen silence.

"Listen to this one, El," Hermit said, picking up the other book. "The day dawned clear, but it had rained the night before, the sudden squally rain of middle March." He looked at Eleanor, asked, "Which one you like best?" conciliation toning his words

El looked at him and cool as a cucumber tossed the half eaten cookie to the duff beside the drooping cedar. She held her stare then jumped from the log and went to the Brule's bank. She stuck her paws in the gentle eddy at the water's edge where she washed her hands of the whole debacle. She splashed water on her face. She lapped a few laps like a cat drinking. She stared at Hermit. She clicked her teeth together three times loudly and waddled away into the forest.

"Be that way," Hermit muttered. Louder, he called after her, "I said thanks, didn't I?"

He repacked his bag. He grunted up off his log and followed the easily offended.

16

"So, Mr. Waldenbillig, what happened yesterday?" Stanski asked.

"Please, call me Leo," the man with a shock of gray hair fashioned in a mullet said. "Thanks for wearing your masks," Leo said through his cloth mask with a large red W screen printed across the front. "I've got bad lungs."

"Anything for a Badgers fan," Stanski said through his N95.

"Too bad they can never finish," Davecki said through his Vikings mask.

"But I love that they don't hire professionals, I mean, it's good that they only recruit true student athletes," Leo said.

"Right," Stanski said.

Waldenbillig flexed his broad shoulders in a tension release.

"So, what happened," Davecki asked.

"I was taking a nap. I was tired from the drive up from Madison to open the cabin. My kids and grandkids are coming for the weekend. I was dreaming about a horse named Milo that could fly. Noise in the living room woke me up. I got up, opened the bedroom door, and there was this big black thing standing by the medicine table. Thought it was a bear at first. Looked like he was going to steal my heart medicine. I spent a few years as an MP in the Navy and a short hitch as a beat cop in Mad Town so I used command voice on him." Leo shook his head.

"What happened?" Stanski asked.

"He froze like I commanded. Then this crazy raccoon attacked me, and he ran out."

"Did the raccoon bite you? You need a rabies shot?"Davecki asked.

"Well, maybe *attack* is too strong," Leo replied. "The little bugger ran at me with bared teeth hissing like a banshee. Scared the daylights out of me," Leo shook his graying head again. "That's when he made a break for it, and they both took off out the back door."

"What went missing?" Stanski asked. He pulled his notebook.

"Canned goods, cookies and books, as far as I can tell," Leo said. "He dropped the aspirin bottle."

"Fits the M.O.," Davecki said.

"You have him patterned already?" Leo asked.

Stanski said, "It's this guy's M.O. to break in, take food and books, and leave more valuable items."

"Don't forget his propensity for propane," Davecki added.

Stanski rolled his eyes. "Don't mind my partner."

Leo looked cross. "I won't."

"Sorry," Davecki said. "It's a disease."

"Anyway," Stanski said, "you can get my report off the website. Were the books valuable?" He handed Waldenbillig a business card.

"Naw. They were good books, but not worth much," Leo said. "It's not like it was a signed copy or anything."

"Mind if we take a look around the property?" Davecki asked.

"No problem," Leo said. "I'm assuming this is the notorious burglar of the Brule I've heard about."

"Most likely," Stanski said.

"You familiar?" Davecki asked.

"We just bought this place last fall. The previous owners didn't say anything, but after the closing, the real estate agent suggested new and better locks."

"Did you?"

"Naw. It's just a cabin," Leo said with a slight smile.

"Okay then. We'll take a look around outside and will check in with you before we leave," Stanski said.

"I'm heading to Superior for groceries. The grandkids eat like horses."

"Okay then," Stanski said.

"Don't forget the cookies," Davecki said.

"First priority," Waldenbillig said with a grin.

"No problem cutting trail this time," Davecki said at the edge of the lawn. He pointed at an alder branch bent back like a compound fracture.

"Big footprint there," Stanski said as they stepped from the lawn to the woods.

Spoor was everywhere. It led them to the swooping cedar by the river. Davecki bent down. He picked up a half-eaten snickerdoodle. "Unlike the Hermit to leave this behind," he displayed the morsel to Stanski who went wide eyed when Davecki chomped on the cookie and said, "A little soggy, but good yet."

"You're eating evidence again, doofus."

"Better me than the mice," Davecki grinned. He popped the remains of the cookie in and smirked. Chewing, he cut a path around the cedar bench, past Stanski, and toward the river. He wove a pattern through the understory beneath the popple-spruce-balsam mix.

Returning to Stanski he said, "No fresh vegetative bruising," he said. "He rested here after his flight response. Once he got it together he resorted to his cautious ways. Hard to tell which direction he went," he said. "But my guess is toward the Winneboujou section."

"Vegetative bruising? Seriously?"

"Hey! I'm a highly trained tracker," Davecki said.

"Flight response?"

"You're the one who wanted me to read the handbook," Davecki said.

Stanski shook his head. "He's good at disappearing."

"Should be called the Phantom of the Brule," Davecki said.

"What now?" Stanski asked.

Davecki studied the forest for the trees. "I'm thinking lunch. That partial cookie made me hungry."

"A true professional," Stanski said.

They headed for the squad.

When the birds started chirping again, Hermit came down from the upper reaches of a huge spruce tree. "Did you hear that, Eleanor? Now I'm the Phantom of the Brule. Cool."

Eleanor waddled to river's edge, ignoring Hermit.

"How long you going to keep pouting?" Hermit asked. "You're

the one who threw down the cookie. You were very brave to confront the man in the cabin. Thank you."

Eleanor watched a leaf floating past on the slow moving water. Silence occupied the space for a full thirty seconds until she showed her teeth in a snarl or a smile. "Chitter-chit," she said. She stuck both front paws in the slow moving water. She washed her hands.

"You know you're sort of OCD with the paw washing, don't you?" Hermit said.

Eleanor turned her masked eyes over her shoulder. She stared while continuing to rub her paws together. "Chitter-chit," she said.

"That's better," Hermit said. He pulled on his beard. He swatted at the sprinkling of green spruce needles decorating the long black whiskers laced with streaks of gray. "We gotta be more careful from now on."

"Chitter-chit."

"Couldn't agree more," Hermit said. "I'm hungry, too."

17

After wolfing down leftover stroganoff, Davecki grabbed an aluminum pie plate, a bag of Cheetos and a baggie half-filled with Oreos. He donned his fisherman's vest, sticking the pound propane tank inside the flap like it was a concealed-carry Glock, only unconcealed. He hiked back to the river. Anything resembling exercise was better than falling asleep in the recliner with Family Feud re-runs on the TV. The trauma of Harry Harrison getting the drop on him sleeping in the recliner made the nap custom far less appealing.

At the river, Davecki found a more-or-less open patch of brush ten yards away from the fisherman's path. He checked for a wood tick nursery and, finding none, deftly distributed the oblations, arranging the propane tank in a pleasing fashion that accented the Cheetos and directed the eye toward the cookies spread out lavishly. Satisfied with the presentation, he took in the surroundings. The water flowed quiet and easy through Scotty O's Riffles. Like Calgon, the gentle breeze took the mosquitoes away. No bird chirped. No distant whir of jetliners descending into Duluth not-really-International. No faraway rumble of heavy pulp and gravel trucks on distant Highway H. No soughing tree tops.

He studied the land rising to the west and began weaving between the trees uphill. As he ascended he looked for an undisclosed location from which to observe, perhaps to catch as catch can, or maybe rule the government in time of crisis. Halfway up the steep bank, a glacial erratic boulder half the size of Stanksi's Ioniq squad suggested a perfect observation post. Sweeping lichen away, taking a closer look for wood ticks and espying none, he sat.

He dozed.

He got uncomfortable and returned to medium alertness to rearrange his backside on the hard rock not café.

"Bonk," came a sound.

What the heck was that? He wondered.

"Bonk," the sound came again.

Davecki looked right. Staggering around through the underbrush, a raccoon. The animal's ringed tail pointed straight up like a meerkat confronting a cobra, its neck stretched out long. On said head, a tin can. "Bonk," the can-head ran into another tree.

"Oh, oh," Davecki whispered. "Hey, Rocky," he called.

The raccoon stopped and crouched. Its tin can head tilted toward Davecki.

"Poor guy," Davecki said. He slid off the rock to his feet.

Raccoon heard the noise and scampered away banging into brush, alder, and sticks.

"Doggone it," Davecki said, initiating pursuit.

The fleeing raccoon rushed head-long, or can-long, away from rescue.

Striding after the scrambling ringtail, Davecki removed his fishing vest.

The raccoon bonked into another moss covered boulder. The tin can clinked. As the raccoon backed away, Davecki tossed his vest, covering the confused coon like a blanket. The vest rustled for a moment. Then the coon's can-adorned head popped out like Sigourney Weaver's alien exploding out of a chest. The world stood still for a moment, and the suddenly animated vest took off across the forest floor like a Roomba vacuuming leaves.

Davecki gave chase again.

Raccoon ran for a ten yard gain and a first down until a linebacker balsam tree grabbed the Roomba-vest with a supple green limb. The balsam tackle flipped the raccoon and vest upside down where the animal lay, breathing heavily, furry legs churning at the sky.

Davecki rushed up and flipped a vest flap over the churning paws to avoid getting clawed and to prevent another first down. The alien under cover of vest settled down.

Moving slow as a cat stalking a mouse, Davecki lowered himself to one knee next to the vest. The vest rustled a little, but settled down with only the coon's struggle for breath raising and lowering the fabric.

One-one-thousand, he counted to himself. At ten-one-thousand, Davecki reached for the can like he was feeling for a light switch at midnight. He ever so lightly put fingers and thumb to the silver bottom of the Bush's Best baked bean can *Original Recipe.* When he got in a good position, he clamped down on the can, twisting and pulling and lifting.

Like a fish on the end of the line, the raccoon dangled, wiggled, and twisted. Black paws clawed at can and air.

Davecki held tight and twisted the can. "Plink!" It came free.

"Snap," the balsam branch entwined with the vest broke as the fat raccoon landed with a thump. Tucking and rolling like a WWII paratrooper landing; Raccoon took off, vest fluttering around the fleeing animal like a hovercraft skittering across the forest floor.

Bush's Best can in hand, Davecki watched the ringtail and his vest scamper away down the embankment.

The broken off balsam branch flopping along with the fleeing Roomba-coon caught in the ground. The stick flexed but did not break, it lifted the vest and raccoon like a pole-vaulter going for Olympic gold. At the apex of the vault, ringtail and vest parted company. The vest swayed at the top of the stick like a flag on a pole. Raccoon skidded to a halt. He or she sat on hefty haunches, looked at Davecki, and rubbed both paws behind both ears. Massaging and smoothing out the hair there, Raccoon gave Davecki two blinks, licked his or her lips, showed some teeth in a smile or a snarl, turned, and waddled away.

"Ingrate," Davecki said. He retrieved his vest, brushed raccoon hair from the webbing. He whacked it hard against a rare yellow birch, checked for ticks, donned it, and stuffed the bean can inside the flap. He looked uphill and down; What in the world am I doing out here? He looked for the blue sky beyond the green leaves. Sometimes I feel like I'm in *The Truman Show,* he thought. Mosquitoes swarmed. Hermit be damned, he thought. I'm heading home. He swished at the mosquitoes. He ripped open a vest pocket, pulled a small spray can of DEET, and fogged himself.

About to take a step north towards home, Raccoon reappeared, beady black eyes blinking.

"What's the matter, Lassie?"

Raccoon half-turned southward and uphill.

"Jimmy's trapped in the well?" Davecki asked.

Raccoon shook his or her head, turned ringtail, and waddled away.

Was that disgust or come hither in its eyes? Davecki pondered the raccoon's message. This could get interesting, he thought, recalling Waldenbillig's raccoon tale. Eschewing home and comfort, he decided to follow the not-yellow brick road.

Leading a human on a bushwhacking track though the trees, shrubs, and burgeoning grasses of early summer requires a lot of patience on a raccoon's part. Ferns in abundance, some tall as second-graders, spread across the shaded landscape like a green woven carpet under which a raccoon vanishes. Davecki followed as best he could, stopping to listen for raccoon steps or to scan the fern-tops for movement like green riffles on a sea of fanning leaves. Sometimes when he lost the track, he got down on hands and knees to scout out the dim underworld below the fern canopy. If that didn't work and he was about to cease and desist, the raccoon would reappear and lead him onward.

Up and down ravines and ridges, around downed pines and glacial erratic boulders with bulging green shoulders covered in lichen and moss, the tracker tracked or the raccoon led. Occasionally Hoodoo Lake appeared at various distances in the valley so low.

Stopping on a hog's back of thick underbrush, Davecki pulled DEET and fogged-up again. He announced, "This is stupid," to a phalanx of Norway pines that rose like Roman columns guarding the temple of black rock behind. He swept at the air to the amusement of hovering mosquitoes.

A Chipping Sparrow joined the party, flittering in from the rock embankment. It landed on a spindly Ironwood branch a mere two feet from Davecki's face. The black beak beneath the orange cap yawned, the following tweet sounded like, "This way. This way." The bird flew back the way it came from, directly toward the cliff face.

Sans raccoon, Davecki said, "Whatever," and followed his new leader.

Sparrow flitted from branch to branch leading Davecki to the vertical rock-face that rose about twenty feet from the forest floor. The rock face looked like a gaunt old haunted house staring through the façade of stout Norway pines standing guard. Like a boreal magic trick, at the base of the mini-cliff, a broad sheet of camo rip-stop tarp appeared, hung from a line of rope stretched from a pine tree to another pine trunk fifteen feet away. Arranged along the curtain bottom, a dozen 20-pound propane tanks sat in dis-order like tumbled bloated bowling pins. Interspersed amongst the tanks, a haphazard array of two-dozen or more red plastic gas cans ranging from one to five gallons added an Andy Warhol artistic feel to the scene. Green grass growing out of the dead leaves and spongy moss surrounding the dumped fossil fuel containers did its best to add a touch of green ecology.

Looks almost natural, Davecki thought.

"Cheep-cheep-cheep," Sparrow's beak flexed, showing a wiggling tongue.

Is that a smile? Davecki wondered.

The bird's bright black eyes glimmered. It stuck out its tongue again, wagged its feathery head and flew around the tarp.

"Hello the camp!" Davecki called.

Rustling behind the camo screen, a stocky man with a black beard stepped into view. Under his right arm the raccoon nestled. On his left shoulder, Ms. Sparrow perched. A wet green washcloth drooped over his left hand. The beard moved. "Miss Sparrow! You bad girl!" the Hermit of the Brule said.

Miss Sparrow chirped at the Hermit.

Davecki wondered, is that feathery indignation I hear?

Miss Sparrow flapped wings and flew away.

Hermit raised the green washcloth to his face, scrubbing with vigor. Speaking as he scrubbed, he said, "Kids these days."

If you say so, Davecki thought.

Hermit ceased his ablutions with a swipe of his arm, using his shirtsleeve as a towel.

Pretty clean looking for a hermit, Davecki thought.

Hermit took a swipe at the raccoon's masked face with the washcloth.

The raccoon squirmed away from the cleansing.

Hermit grabbed the squirmer by the nose, using the washcloth as a muzzle. He bent the furry head to the side as the raccoon hissed and gurgled. Cooing like a mom checking to see if her offspring had washed behind its ears, he said, "She got stuck in a can again, didn't she?"

Davecki produced the Bush's Best can.

Hermit released his grip on her face. He held her by the body with both hands, extending her at arms length. "Eleanor! I told you a hundred times not to stick your nose into cans." He shook his shaggy head.

Suspended as if in a Jolly Jumper baby sling, Eleanor clawed the air, chittering a loud complaint, all four limbs twirling like pinwheels in a strong wind.

"Settle down, you!" Hermit said. He made a kind of half toss that landed the dervish raccoon on his shoulder.

Eleanor twisted around like Suni Lee taking up a surveillance position on Hermit's shoulder, eying the intruder with beady black orbs radiating contempt or suspicion or maybe admiration at Davecki's ability to keep up and follow.

Davecki swished at the gathering mosquitoes. "Why aren't the bugs bugging you?" he asked.

"I eat right," Hermit said.

"You want me to wear a mask?" Davecki asked.

Hermit swished the green washcloth in Davecki's direction dismissively. Snorting like Sandra Bullock in *Miss Congeniality,* he ignored the question with, "Would you like some tea?"

"Sounds good," Davecki said, shrugging his shoulders. He pulled his mini spray can of DEET out and, like the war on drugs, fought a losing battle.

Following the Hermit behind the camo tarp, Davecki saw a four-inch thick slab of white pine that had been hand hewn with an adz, the adz scallops still visible along the relatively flat surface that Hermit tossed the washcloth to. The tabletop was supported on two legs thirty inches tall and thick as five-quart ice cream pails. The other end of the six-foot long table rested on a squat, flat-faced boulder that could have been a blank for an Easter Island maoi statue. The table's edges were worn smooth from use. Atop the table, an Anne Hillerman paperback rested. An empty tea bag packet acted as a bookmark protruded from the middle of the book's pages. Beside the Hillerman a battered Coleman two-burner camp stove held an aluminum pot whose black bottom had seen more than its fair share of open flames. From the pot, steam.

Did he know company was coming? Davecki wondered.

"Have a seat," Hermit said. He reached one arm up like he was going to pull a shirt over his head. Instead he grabbed Eleanor by the scruff of her fluffy neck. "Down you go," he said. He lifted Eleanor.

Eleanor had other ideas. She dug her nails into Hermit's Stormy Kromer shirt. "Be nice," Hermit said as he levitated the clingy ball of fur.

"Squeak!" Eleanor complained. She clung to the wool with crafty claws. Her legs stretched out like furry bungee cords. She swung her pointed nose toward Hermit's heavy hand, nipping with gleaming white teeth.

"Chica mala," Hermit said. "Bad girl," he translated, pulling harder.

"Squeak!" Eleanor yelped as she lost the battle against the Hermit's superior pulling power. Her claws popped out of the heavy fabric. Torn threads dangled. As Hermit swung Eleanor away, she made a last grab for her hero's head. Hermit ducked away, but too late. Eleanor's sharp claws snatched away the Stormy Kromer cap on Hermit's head.

That would be Oliver O'Grady's Kromer, Davecki reasoned.

"Chica mala!" he repeated, reaching for his hat.

"Chitter chitter," Eleanor uttered from the back of her throat as her incisors held firm to the hat's brim.

The two did battle over the black and red checked hat. Bent at the waist as he did battle with the raccoon, Davecki could see the slight-light glowing of a nascent bald patch starting in the Hermit's bountiful crop of black hair. The black hair on the sides of his head looked like strands of rope falling over his ears.

Reminds me of Friar Tuck, Davecki thought. Wish I could get a picture; Stanski will never believe this. He ripped open the Velcro vest pocket, extracting his phone.

Hermit pulled the Stormy Kromer up and up until Eleanor's back feet were off the ground. She dangled there, the hat acting like a woolen tow strap, until, letting go, she plopped to the ground. Hermit rose, put the hat on his head, said, "I win!"

Eleanor waddled away with a hiss, casting a scurrilous glance over her shoulder at the still grinning Hermit. She flopped over onto the packed earth floor and regarded the humans.

Seeing the phone, Hermit said, "No signal here, friend, and no photos," his brow furrowed.

"Sorry," Davecki said, "I was thinking a video of you and your raccoon fighting over a Stormy Kromer would go viral on TikTok."

"Sorry," Hermit said, "no dice." A deadly look came into his eyes that convinced Davecki to repocket the device. "What's TikTok?"

"A video app," Davecki said.

"Another modern convenience I will gladly do without," Hermit said. Adjusting the hat, he looked at Eleanor, added, "She's a good girl, but not to be trusted." He snuck a glance at Davecki.

"She doesn't usually bring strays home?" Davecki asked.

"The occasional brook trout but never the upright and two-legged type." Hermit turned toward the rock wall four feet behind him where a natural shelf of black basalt held a flat tin box with a Currier and Ives Christmas scene printed on the cover. Hermit boosted the black box. He pushed a yellow brass button in the facia.

The lid popped up. "It's about Earl Grey time, don't you think? Green lacks the punch the mid-afternoon slump requires."

"Sounds good," Davecki said as he took a seat on a stool that was more than a stool. It was a tree stump, being eighteen inches in diameter and two feet tall. Atop the chunk of pine, a blaze orange vinyl deer hunter's Hot Seat identical to one Davecki owned. Where'd he steal this from? Davecki wondered.

Hermit tossed two Earl Gray tea packets to the table, clicked the tea tin shut and tucked it back onto the natural rock shelf from which he grabbed a mug that rested amidst numerous salt and pepper shakers and an assortment of spices and small bottles with hand printed labels.

Wonder how many break-ins that collection required, Davecki thought.

The light blue mug in Hermit's heavy hand had a black poodle silk-screened on the exterior. Hermit blew into the poodle cup. A leaf the size of a quarter flew up from within. "Huh," he said.

Ugh, no mask, no social distancing, airborne transmission: good thing I'm vaccinated, boostered, and nano-tagged, Davecki thought.

Hermit inverted the cup. He knocked it against the table top. He looked back into the cup's depths. "Persistent are we?" He stuck his wizened finger into the cup. He scraped a dirty fingernail inside. Inverting the cup, he again knocked it against the table. Looking into the cup again he said, "That's better."

The orange Japanese beetle evicted from the cup, scuttered away across the tabletop.

"Do you know the difference between black and green tea?" Hermit asked.

"Can't say that I do," Davecki reached out to squash the beetle.

"No!" Hermit said. "Every living thing!"

Davecki retracted his finger of death.

The beetle vanished under the green Coleman two burner stove.

The two of them looked at the stove in silence until Hermit pulled the brass fuel tank pumping-rod out of the filler hole and, pumping the pressure up like he was inflating a bicycle tire, answered his own question, "There is no difference. They're the same leaves, only green tea is processed to prevent more oxidization."

"I see," Davecki Lamotted.

"To what do we owe the honor of your presence today?" Hermit continued the small talk.

Well, I was wondering where you stole the camp stove, Davecki thought. "That's an old stove," he said. "Where do you get white gas anymore?"

"Unleaded works," Hermit said.

Stolen from how many Brule garages, Davecki thought, a vision of the discarded gas cans out front playing on his mind screen.

Hermit dragged a white mug with *Midland Services* silk screened on the outside across the table. The mug was stained black at the bottom, the dirt and dark fading as it rose past the red lettering. At the rim, the stain was visible all around except where pure white showed, indicating that bearded lips had been drinking for days, weeks, months, perhaps decades with nary a wash. He put the tea bags in the cups. "Always pour the water over the bag," Hermit said as if repeating a sacred religious mantra. "So, you're just out for a day hike?"

"I was out setting up a bait station to lure you in for questioning," Davecki answered. "When your raccoon appeared with her head in a can I managed to catch her and get her free." Davecki picked up the bean can, spinning it in his fingers.

Hermit scowled at Eleanor. "I figured it was you who stole my beans."

They would be the O'Grady's beans, Davecki thought.

Eleanor looked away, resembling a scolded dog.

"You're lucky Mr. Davecki found you."

He knows my name, Davecki thought.

Eleanor laid her lower jaw flat on the well-packed ground. She looked from Davecki to Hermit rolling her eyes in her head like a mechanical doll. She showed her teeth.

"An endearing smile will do you no good," Hermit said. "I'm staying mad at you." He poured steaming water from the pot to the cups. Splashes of water missed the cups making little puddles on the tabletop.

Davecki could see into the open pot as the Hermit poured. At the bottom, tiny strands of sand and bits of black shards shifted around the bottom like waves moved by the clear water flowing.

Hermit replaced the two quart pot. He grabbed the handle of another similar sized pot on the two burner camp stove. "I made some nice stew. Would you like some?"

"I am hungry," Davecki said, "very kind of you."

"No problem. It says in Hebrews to entertain strangers, in so doing you may be entertaining angels unawares."

I'm no angel, Davecki thought. "That's a compliment," he said.

"I was thinking of the stranger part."

I wonder why everyone seems to think I'm strange, Davecki thought. "Thanks—I think," he said.

Twisting the valve to shut the flames under the water pot off, Hermit pumped up pressure again and lit the burner under the stew with a snout-nosed lighter.

Sure does have a lot of modern amenities for a hermit, Davecki thought.

Hermit tended to his tea. He looked at the raccoon lying on its belly still keeping an eye on the humans. "Okay El, I'm not mad at you anymore," he said.

"That was fast," Davecki said.

"'Be gentle and quick to forgive; never hold grudges,' it says in Colossians," Hermit said.

Eleanor grinned again.

"Doesn't the Bible say it's not good for man to be alone?" Davecki asked. "Sorta makes being a hermit unchristian doesn't it?"

"Jesus sent everyone away and went alone to the mountains to pray in secret," Hermit said.

"I can see I'm no match for you with Scripture," Davecki said.

"Four years in Seminary will do that," Hermit said.

Duly noted, Davecki thought. He wrapped both hands around the hot mug. "After I got her head out of her can she acted like I was supposed to follow her."

Hermit snorted again. His thick black moustache jumped like a furry vole under his bulbous nose, a bit of yellow mucus slooped out of his left nostril and landed on the vole's back. "Me thinks thou dost assumed too much, officer Davecki."

"How do you know my name?" Davecki asked.

Hermit, with elbow on table and right hand raising and dipping, raising and dipping his tea bag in the steaming cup of water, sniffed again. The mucus retreated from the vole's back, returning to its nasal hidey-hole. "It's on your mailbox, sir."

Can't argue with that, Davecki thought. "And you know I'm an officer of the law?"

"Retired," Hermit added. He picked up a silver spoon. He caught his tea bag in the spoon's bowl. He wrapped the bag's string around the spoon and bag. He tightened the string, squeezing a goodly stream of hot brown tea from bag to cup. To finish the job, he pressed his thumb into the bag extracting even more tea.

"And you know I'm retired how?" Davecki asked. He sipped. "Nice tea," he said. "Thanks."

"Don't thank me; thank a slave laborer in the tea fields of China," Hermit said. "You know it is bad form to drink tea with the bag still in the cup, don't you?"

"Never knew that," Davecki said. He commenced to imitating Hermit's bag protocol.

Watching Davecki squeeze his bag, Hermit said, "You catch on fast."

"Irritation is the sincerest form of flattery," Davecki said.

"Isn't that *imitation*?" Hermit asked.

Davecki set his spoon and squashed tea bag aside. "Normally, but Stanski and I have brought the insult and pun game to a higher level."

"Ah yes, Officer Deer Striker, he of the demolished squad car." Hermit's shoulders heaved in humor.

Guy gets around, Davecki thought.

Hermit adjusted the stew pot.

More stolen property, no doubt, Davecki thought.

Hermit sipped more tea. He smiled. He sighed a satisfied sigh. "Nailed it," he said. "Life is like a cup of tea," he said. "It's all in how you make it."

"Can't argue with that," Davecki said. He asked again, "How do you know I'm retired?"

"All the AARP promos in your mailbox. You learn a lot about people investigating their mailboxes."

"Mail tampering is a federal offense," Davecki said.

"I never tamper. Opening a neighbor's mailbox is not a crime."

We're neighbors? Davecki thought. "Even reading a return address could be considered tampering," Davecki said.

Hermit huffed, "In whose court of law? You shouldn't leave mail in your box overnight if you value your privacy."

One never knows what's going on in the middle of the night in rural Wisconsin, Davecki thought. "Can't argue with that," he said.

They drank. A gentle gust of wind whispered through between the rock wall and the camo sheet pushing away the mosquitoes hovering around Davecki. The breeze carried the Ode du Hermit fragrance to Davecki's nose. He doesn't smell that bad, he thought. Like a cross between a mouse dead in a trap for a day and a half in summer, combined with the roasted nutty scent of dark chocolate.

"Nice place you got here," Davecki said.

"Very serene," Hermit said.

"Sorta hard to find," Davecki said.

"Next thing to impossible," Hermit said, "if it weren't for her." He nodded at Eleanor. Her chin was now flat on the ground, both eyes closed in repose. At her name she opened one eyelid, studied the humans a bit and closed the eye, perhaps to dream. Hermit looked at Davecki. "On your own recognizance you'd never have found it, am I correct?"

"Can't argue with that," Davecki said.

"Based on your frequent use of the phrase, I assume you came here to argue something?" Hermit asked.

"No. No. Just a figure of speech," Davecki said.

"Or Freudian," Hermit said.

"You sound like Stanski," Davecki said.

"How does he like his new squad car?" Hermit asked.

"Not thrilled," Davecki answered. Wonder how much he knows about Stan, he thought.

"So, this seems like a pretty sparse living arrangement," Davecki said.

Hermit sipped tea. His blue eyes studied Davecki over the rim of his Midland Services cup. The cup's red lettering matched the tiny red blood vessels in the Hermit's sclera. "This is just my tea room. Your interview style leans to indirectness," he said.

"As do your answers, Davecki said. "I can be more direct if you prefer."

"What do *you* prefer?" Hermit asked.

That you'd answer a question directly, Davecki thought. "I favor directness."

"As do I," Hermit said. A trace of a smile may have occurred behind the whiskers that covered his lips. "Shall we give it a try?"

Are his lips even moving? Davecki wondered. The speech seemed more to emerge from the bushy beard than come out pronounced by mouth, tongue, and lips.

"Can't hurt," Davecki said. "What's your name?"

"Huh," Hermit answered, "I was actually talking about trying the stew. It should be ready by now." He went to the rock wall cupboard, picking up two bowls. He blew in them and set them on the table. He retrieved two oversized spoons. One he plunked in the bowl closest to Davecki. With the other he stirred the pot.

"You have another hidey-hole somewhere nearby?" Davecki asked.

"I've already said too much on that matter."

"At least you're direct with your indirectness," Davecki said. "Refusing to identify yourself to a peace officer is grounds for arrest."

"Are you detaining me, Officer?"

"No, just having a friendly discussion."

"All good attorneys advise against talking to the police unless a lawyer is present."

"Are you a lawyer?"

"Not anymore. Seminary then law school then in service to the church then tossed aside."

"Well then," Davecki said, "I guess it won't do any good to be direct and ask if you burgled the O'Grady cabin last week and took his Stormy Kromer and Anne Hillerman book." Davecki looked at each item as he mentioned them.

Again with the snort. Mr. Mucus stayed hidden. "If you're referring to this," Hermit touched the bottom of his cup to the book, "and this," he lifted cup toward the brim of his Stormy Kromer, "I found both these items in a ditch alongside Highway 97." He sipped his tea. The hint of a gleam splintered from his penetrating blue eyes.

Liar, Davecki thought. "How convenient," he said.

"The Lord provides in mysterious ways his miracles to perform."

"I take it you're no longer a priest or a lawyer?" Davecki asked.

Hermit gazed into his tea cup as if there were lawyerly leaves at the bottom advising on an answer. "True to some extent," he said. "Maybe it's like the Marines, once a priest, always a priest?"

His answer conveyed uncertainty. Davecki wondered if he'd found a crack in the rock. "Why become a hermit?"

"As a Franciscan it gets me in touch with animals and nature with the additional benefit of freedom from church and the world's foibles."

Davecki sipped his tea. Foibles indeed, Davecki thought. There's more to the story. He decided to press. "Let me guess. Defrocked?"

Hermit glanced at Davecki, snuck a look at sleeping Eleanor to disguise the slight scowl. "Close," he said.

Now who's being indirect, Davecki thought.

Hermit scanned the woods behind Davecki's back. "All have sinned," he said. He sighed. "Luckily Christ died for everyone's sins." He sipped tea.

"How about this?" Davecki asked. "Why did you break and enter

Leo Waldenbillig's cabin two days ago?"

"Another bon mot is, 'Never a why question unless your lawyer is present,'" Hermit replied.

That's a yes, Davecki thought.

Hermit's shoulders hunched again, this time though, it was in time with a chuckle-laugh that produced Mr. Mucus again. He rubbed the snot away with his index finger. He dried the finger on his wool pants. He pulled a cookie from its packet. Hermit asked, "Would you like a snickerdoodle?"

At the word snickerdoodle, Eleanor's jaw came off the floor.

This is getting old, Davecki thought. "No thanks."

"Suit yourself," Hermit said. He tossed the proffered cookie to Eleanor. She grabbed it in mid-air like Hank Aaron chasing down a fly ball at County Stadium. He fetched a second cookie for himself.

Davecki drank. He swallowed and asked, "How about this? Last weekend did you pull Mercy Madigan out from under the water on Hall Rapids, disarm her, and throw her three-thousand dollar Colt Python in the river, thus committing felony grand theft?"

"I never go on the river on the weekends. Too many idiots drinking beer, blasting stereos, disturbing the peace."

Davecki drank more tea. "I assume you're aware of what I speak. Or at least it seems as if," he said.

"Assuming makes an ass out of you and me," Hermit said.

Sounds like Kaylee Remington, Davecki recalled the young musher. He said, "I don't suppose you'd be willing to enter custody voluntarily and come in for further questioning."

"Are you detaining me, Officer?" Hermit showed a bit of yellowed teeth behind the drooping Sam Elliot mustache.

"I have a reasonable suspicion that you have committed crimes." Davecki tapped the Hillerman with the bottom of his poodle cup. He eyeballed the hat.

"Picking up litter is not a crime."

Davecki sighed. "True." He finished his tea. "Lying to a peace officer is."

"So, you're detaining me?"

No backup out here, Davecki thought.

"Are you arresting me?"

Geeze, who is this guy and where did he go to law school? Davecki thought. He said, "No," adding, "the tea is going right through me. I've got to tinkle."

"Have at it," Hermit said. He shut the burner under the stew off and commenced to spooning stew to Davecki's bowl.

While Davecki was beyond the camo tarp, Hermit went to the basalt cupboard. He picked up a hand-labeled spice-type jar. He returned to the table, ladled stew to a bowl, unscrewed the black cap on the spice jar. He sprinkled a liberal amount of flakes into Davecki's stew and stirred it in. He capped the jar, stuck it in his coat pocket and ladled stew to a bowl of his own.

Davecki returned. "That used to happen a lot quicker twenty years ago," he said.

"Tell me about it," Hermit said. "Growing old is not for the faint of heart."

Eating, Davecki said, "This is delicious. What's in it?"

"It's slug stew," Hermit said. "I got the recipe from a Duluth dirt lady cookbook."

The spoon making its way from bowl to Davecki's mouth may have faltered slightly.

Hermit may have raised his eyebrows slightly.

Davecki may have said, that's disgusting, but instead he said, "Very tasty," and kept eating.

"So, back to the issue at hand," Hermit said. "Are you going to arrest me for refusing to produce identification?"

"Are you willing to come along peacefully?"

"I'm committed to non-violence. But Eleanor might object."

Shades of Leo Waldenbillig, Davecki thought. "I'm not up to fighting a raccoon," he retreated. He clinked his spoon into his empty bowl at the bottom of which a happy face announced, ALL DONE!

"So, then? Is there anything else?" Hermit asked.

Davecki picked up the Hillerman book. He opened to the half

title page. *Well met in Manotowash, Oliver. Anne Hillerman.* Davecki snuck a glance at the Stormy Kromer, made a quick decision to eschew hat and said, "Nothing more. Oliver will be real happy to get his lost book back."

"I'm only half way through."

"Funny, he said the same thing." Davecki pulled the tea packet bookmark from the pages. He tossed the marker to the table, observing the flare of anger rising in Hermit's eyes. He stuck the book under the flap of his fishing vest.

Hermit said nothing.

"Maybe he'll loan it back to you when he's done. If you ask nice."

Hermit's face settled down. The anger in the air evaporated. "If I get over that way, I'll see if they're home and ask nice," he emphasized the "ask nice" bit.

"Good idea," Davecki said. "It's always best to ask for permission rather than forgiveness."

"I think it's the other way around," Hermit said.

"Really? If you say so," Davecki said. He studied the SK hat. "I'm thinking that's his hat too."

Hermit removed the hat. He inverted it, looking at the hat's band. "I see no identifying marks," he raised his eyes, challenge streaming like flung daggers at Davecki.

Not worth it, Davecki thought. "Right," he said. He turned away heading for, he hoped, the way home.

"Enjoy your walk," Hermit called after.

18

Fifteen or twenty minutes later, or maybe an hour or a day later as far as Davecki knew, he put his hand against a popple tree the diameter of an old-time wringer washing machine. He wondered... why are the trees dancing to Lawrence Welk music? He looked up, the green canopy above blinked to pink, then blue. What in the world...? He looked at his hand against the be-bopping tree. What a nice hand, he thought. A nice tree. He spread his fingers. He drummed them against the bark the way Stanski drummed his steering wheel. Stan...such a nice man-Stan. He moved his palm around against the bark. Nice bark. Bark so nice. Davecki leaned into the tree; he wrapped his arms around it. "Mom," he muttered as he hugged and hugged. He leaned back. He looked up the tree trunk. "I love you, mom," he said. He kissed the tree and looked up again, tipping his head back until he fell backwards, landing in a heap.

Looking up at the bottom side of ferns, he said, "Hello Ferns. Such nice Ferns."

It was cool in the shade...cool ground. He struggled to get himself backed up against Mother Popple. He picked up the fallen Hillerman book. He pulled his phone out. No signal. He scooted his butt around grinding out a smoother surface. He leaned his head back against Mother Tree. "Such a nice tree," he said. He put the phone down. He picked up a dried leaf. He lifted the leaf to his face. He studied the leaf, one side and the other. With his free finger he traced the veins and outline of the leaf. "You are fearfully and wonderfully made little leaf," he said. He picked a wood tick off his pants leg. "Nice little ticky-wicky," he said as he gently put it on the leaf and set both aside.

He leaned his head back against Mother Tree and sighed. "What a wonderful world this would be," he mumbled. He closed his eyes and hummed Armstrong's famous melody. He looked around, "I see trees of green...and a raccoon?" He tried to focus on the greater world around him, but beyond his toes all was wavy and blurry. As Eleanor crept closer she came into sharper focus. "Huh," he said. He reached out toward her as his jaw lowered and his hand lowered and he fell asleep.

Eleanor tip-toed in, walked up the drugged sleeper's lap, grabbed the Hillerman, put it in her teeth and took off running.

Someone snoring loudly irritated Davecki and ruined his second dream in as many days of flying over the beautiful Brule valley. The snoring got even louder and woke him. He lifted up his eyes unto the hills. He wiped drool from his chin and blinked and looked around and saw a wood tick crawling up the leg of his blue jeans that might have been blue, purple, or pink. He flicked the tick off with a snap of his index finger. He stood up, patted the tree, said, "Thanks, Mom," and wandered away.

He didn't see the forest for the trees, but he did see Angel Kelly who saved him from freezing to death and being shot to death in, maybe, a previous life. "Hey, Kelly!" he hollered. "Wait up!"

Kelly smiled at him, waved her arm signifying follow, and glided through the trees like she had a bit part in an M. Night Shyamalan movie.

Cool, Davecki thought. He broke a major rule when lost in the woods. He took off running after his guiding gliding guardian angel. The next thing he knew he was looking up into Kelly's face. "Dave, Dave, Dave," she said. "What are we going to do with you?"

"Umm. Hi, Kell. You here to transport me to the mother ship?"

"We tried that once and you came back here because a woman kissed you," Kelly said.

"Yeah, that was cool," Davecki said with a sigh.

"Repudiating gifts is not good for the soul, David," Kelly said.

"Yeah, it's a bad habit I guess," he answered.

"Maybe it is time to beam me up to the Enterprise," Davecki said.

"This isn't Star Trek, David."

Kelly vanished when he felt a tingling on his calf. He sat up.

He pulled up his pants leg. A brown spider stopped its trek across his white flesh. Davecki flicked a fickle finger of fate at the spider, sending it sailing away. A red two-hole bite glowed against his white flesh, a gift of the spider. Sitting on the forest floor, he looked in the direction where the spider flew. A raccoon sat on its haunches looking back at him.

"You!" he said.

"Chitter-chit."

"Tell your master he's going down," Davecki said.

He thought he heard, "Eleanor master. Hermit slave."

Raccoons don't talk, he thought. "Huh," he said. He shrugged his shoulders. His clavicles cracked. "Huh, huh, huh," he said. Standing, he looked up. This time the leafy canopy, not the sky above, reminded him of *The Truman Show.*

Lacking the sun's position, he pivoted in a slow circle. He took a line of sight on two stately trees. "Thank you, God, for trees," he yelled. He raised his hands and danced in a little circle, kicking up leaves and sticks. "Thank you, God, for trees!" he shouted his praise. As he danced like no one was watching, his phone flew out of its vest pocket.

Spider venom bringing a bit of sobriety to his mushroomed body he suddenly felt shy for some reason. He coughed. He slapped himself on the chin. He tramped through the wavy fern sea, not deviating from his tangent on the God provided popples. The gift of the popples, giving him a raison d'être.

As he vanished into the underbrush, Hermit crossed the dance floor and picked up the phone. "Maybe this guy's not that big a threat, eh El?" he said to the raccoon who was climbing up the raggedy wool pants. Once Eleanor was all the way to the shoulder, she settled in and said, "Chitter, chit chitter."

"Anything you say, bossy," Hermit said. He commenced to following Davecki.

Despite being only semi-conscious of it, Davecki managed to stick to his plan. His meager grip on reason returned in stages as he left the dense fern carpet behind, stuck to sighting trees in a line through the hazel and honeysuckle brush, until coming upon a whitetail path. At the wilderness intersection, he paused for further consideration.

The deer trail angled away from his intended path wandering through wilderness for what? Forty Years? He stood at the intersection. He studied the deer trail. He looked at the two distant trees he had committed to aligning with. Deer trails, he thought, those lazy critters often follow a more or less straight line going to or from whomever puts out the biggest piles of corn on a given day. Should I follow the deer trail or the line of sight? Wish I had a Magic 8-Ball, he thought. He looked at the popple tree he'd stopped by. Can't do paper-scissors-rock with a tree. He reached for his phone. "Dang!" he said.

He picked up a dead popple leaf. He licked it wet on one side. He held it above his head by the stem. He said, "Wet side, deer trail. Dry, popple trees."

Like Liam Neeson in *Clash of the Titans,* Davecki released the kraken leaf.

Leaf spiraled and flipped downward in slow motion. Davecki blinked back awe and wonder at the leaf's languid descent. Leaf decided on doing a triple-tuck, inward-pike, reverse somersault worthy of Greg Louganis, landing dry side up at the toes of his Blackwing boots. He blinked as what appeared to be a wavy, indistinct hand of an angel flipping the leaf over to wet side up.

"Huh," he said. "Deer trail it is," he said. "Crazy," he said, shaking his head and twisting his neck to uncomfortable levels attempting to straighten out his thinking and regain additional layers of rationality.

Watching from the trees a concealed distance away, Hermit said, "Guy really is a strange one, eh, El?"

"Chitter-chit," Eleanor agreed.

When the pathfinder on the deer slayer trail came to an old logging railroad grade, the last of the Mohicans followed the straight and narrow grade to an overgrown snowmobile trail that led to a two rut road that looked familiar and ended in the Shroud of Turin-around driveway of the O'Grady place complete with Oliver O'Grady contributing to global warming gliding across the most expensive lawn in northern Wisconsin on a gleaming green John Deere zero-turn mower.

Seeing an intruder hiking down the not-yellow-brick-road, O'Grady steered the mower toward the turn-around. He shut the ozone killer down at the edge of the black boulders ringing the driveway and dismounted. "You don't look so good," he said when he recognized Davecki.

"I'll live," Davecki said, "especially if I could get a glass of water."

On the porch, laying eyes upon Davecki, Sarah O'Grady said, "Oh, dear. You need a whole bottle of calamine for those bug bites."

Oliver came out of the cabin-cottage-lodge handing Davecki a Daphne Blake glass dappled with condensation on the outside and clinking with ice cubes on the inside.

"Rank roo," Davecki said, slugging water.

"Oh, you're so cute," Sarah said.

"Don't bother with calamine," Oliver O'Grady said. "I'll get the DMSO."

"That junk?" Sarah said. She looked at her hubby. "Snake oil."

"It's the real deal," O'Grady said. "I'll be right back." He scooted back inside.

"What on earth are you doing out on foot in the woods all alone?" Sarah asked.

"Doing something about the Hermit of the Brule," Davecki said.

The slim dark eyebrows on the Mona Lisa face rose. "Really? Any luck? What? Err, why? Err, how did you end up here?"

I was drugged and then led by the grace of God, he thought. "I got turned around," he said.

The Mr. returned with a small white bottle. "Open your palm," O'Grady said to Davecki.

Davecki set Daphne on the cedar balustrade and palms upped.

O'Grady flipped open the nozzle of the three inch tall bottle. He squirted liquid into Davecki's hands. "Rub that around your bites," he said. "This stuff is great."

"Poppycock," the Mrs. said.

"Don't listen to her," the Mr. said.

"Don't listen to *him*," she said nodded at Oliver. She nodded at Davecki, "He was out looking for the hermit."

Davecki rubbed the great-or-not stuff around his face and neck.

"Good luck with that," the Mr. said. "But thanks for trying," he added.

Davecki finished rubbing the medicine, or not, on the back of his neck. "I actually did find him."

"Seriously?" the Mr. and Mrs. said simultaneously.

"How?" the Mr. asked.

"A raccoon with a tin can on its head led me."

"Wow," the Mrs. said.

"What'd he say?" the Mr. asked.

"Raccoons don't talk. At least not to me," Davecki lied again.

O'Grady's face wrinkled to a frown. "You know what I meant."

"Don't be so mean, Ollie," Sarah said.

"I apologize. I have a penchant for joking," Davecki said.

"I'm laughing on the inside," Oliver said.

Davecki said, "As far as the Hermit goes: He refused to tell me his name, but he was a lawyer once. And a priest."

"I'd say he's going up in the world leaving those jobs," Oliver said.

"Oh, Ollie," Sarah said.

"Wondering if you'd mind giving me a ride home," Davecki asked.

"Of course," Ollie said.

Hermit watched the old Bronco glide past his cover of thick alder and balsam. "He's safe now, El."

"Chitter-chit. Chit, chat, chit."

"I agree. Let's go see what he left for bait. Cookies I bet."

"Nice old Bronco," Davecki said.

"Yeah, my dad bought one of the first ones out in sixty-five. He drove it into the ground. I brought it back from the dead," Oliver said.

Steering the Bronc around the numerous mud holes in C Squared Road, Oliver, with his striking shock of white hair said, "I'm worried about Mercy. She's reminding me of the bad old days."

"I see," Davecki didn't.

"It wouldn't surprise me if she has an episode."

"What's that mean?" Davecki asked.

"Not exactly sure, but it won't be good," Oliver said. He glanced at Davecki. He turned right on Cleverton Road. "Some sort of psychotic break. In the past she's done everything from catatonia to hyper paranoia."

"Maybe she has Huntington's," Davecki said.

"If she does, it's undiagnosed," Oliver said.

"Day-paddling with a three-fifty-seven. Seems a little paranoid to me," Davecki said.

"I rest my case," Oliver said. He slowed the Bronco as it crested the road over the escarpment. The miles wide view of the verdant hills and forest spread grandly to the blue jewel of Lake Superior beyond. "Never get tired of this view," he said.

Davecki said, "You and me both."

As the Bronco rolled down the hill and the inspirational view turned into just another road less traveled, Davecki said, "You think she's.... I mean, if she's got mental health issues, you think it's safe for her to be packing in public?"

"It's her second amendment right," Oliver said. He didn't look at Davecki.

Yeah, Davecki thought, but is the public safe? "Granted," he said, "that doesn't answer my question."

O'Grady huffed. "You'll have to ask her."

I will, Davecki thought. "Take a right here," he said.

"I know," O'Grady said as he steered the Bronco into Davecki's driveway.

You do? Davecki thought. I should tell him I had his Hillerman. But then, on the other hand, I'm not even sure I had it in the first place. If I tell him about the book he'll ask me what happened to it. Wish I could remember for sure.

Watching the Bronco depart Davecki shook his head, shaking off the hangover effects of the hallucinogen. Note to self, he thought going inside, never, ever, ever eat slug stew again.

19

"You look like you have the measles," Stanski said. He sank a fork tine into a thick filet of white fish flesh on his plate, cutting it in half. "Why didn't you bring him in? You were right there face to face with him. It would have been nice to get him into custody."

"Well, yah, but his raccoon would have fought me; no way do I want rabies shots."

Stanski held up a forkful of fish, "Let me get this straight, this is lawyer?" He popped the filet in his mouth.

"Yep," Davecki said, forking a chunk off his own filet.

"Why do they call burbot lawyer around these parts?" Stanski asked.

"You have to ask?"

Stanski gave Davecki squint-eye, said, "You always have to answer a question with a question?"

"Oh, sorry," Davecki said, "didn't know my sense of humor offends you. The direct answer is that burbot is an eel that is slippery and slimy. Draw your own inferences. It's also called poor man's lobster."

"Sweet," Stanski said. He looked at the faux crustacean held up on the end of his fork. "This is living the life, man, poor man's lobster for breakfast." He put the morsel in his mouth. "Umm-good," Stanski said. "When you catch it?" he said around his food.

"Like I have time to go fishing any more, chasing around with you on fool's errands. When I got home it was in the fridge. Seagull must have dropped it off."

"Sweet," Stanski said, "Haven't seen Seagull around for a while. How's he doing?"

"I haven't seen him since the Harrison case," Davecki said.

Forking in another bite, Stanski chewed and said, "Must be nice to have a personal bodyguard like that raccoon."

"No kidding. Easy to be committed to non-violence when a wild animal is ready to defend you tooth and claw," Davecki said. A vague, swirling memory of feeling Eleanor climbing up his legs and standing on his belly swished past his mind screen.

Stanski asked, "You think you can find his hidey-hole again?"

"Not sure," Davecki said. "He must have put some sort of mushroom in the slug stew. I was way out of it. Lucky to find the O'Grady place before dark." A vague, swirling memory of an angel beckoning him passed his mind screen.

"You ate slug stew?"

"I was hungry. It was good."

"You're always hungry."

"The kettle calling the pot black," Davecki said. "I know I could find where I left the bait out by Hall Rapids but beyond that, not so much."

"You know what that means, don't you?" Stanski asked. He squeezed his lemon slice on the burbot.

"No."

"You were Hall-lucinating."

"You're a sick individual; you know that, don't you?"

"So I've been told," Stanski said. A bit of fish flesh flew from his lips. It landed on the round oak table. He poked the ort with his finger. Returned it to his mouth. He swallowed and said, "You're going to have to get a new phone now, I suppose."

Davecki said, "I busted my butt fixing you burbot and you ruin it by putting lemon on it."

"I repent. Slide the drawn butter over," Stanski said.

Davecki pushed the ramekin toward Stanski, but not far.

"Jerk," Stanski said. He leaned over the table, stabbed his fork into the small bowl, pulling it to his side.

Davecki laughed. "You're welcome." He drank some chocolate milk.

"How can you stand to drink that stuff with fish?"

Davecki ignored the question, said, "All our Hermit of the Brule troubles are about to be over, Stan."

Stanski eyeballed Davecki. "How so?"

"He has my phone. We use Find My Phone, locate him, you arrest him, case closed, we go trolling for salmon off Houghton Point," Davecki said.

"If you wouldn't or couldn't arrest him, how am I supposed to accomplish it?" Stanski asked.

"We'll get Warden Wendy to help," Davecki said.

"She's tough. That would work," Stanski said.

"Let me see your phone."

Stanski pulled his phone from his duty belt. He slid it just past the ramekin.

"Jerk," Davecki said as he reached across the table with his fork, stabbing the phone and dragging it back.

"Easy on the technology!" Stanski yelped.

"That's what your Otter Box is for, Stan," Davecki answered as he poked and stroked the phone. "What's your password?"

"I'm not telling you that."

"I'm going to have to kill you, Stan."

"Geeze, lighten up, Dave. Seven-eight-two-six-six-nine."

Davecki poked and stroked while Stanski chewed and "Ummed" over the fish. "What you doing to my phone?" Stanski asked.

"Using Find my Phone," Davecki said. "I can't believe it."

"What?"

"I'm beginning to foster a sincere dislike for Mr. Hermit," Davecki said, stroking the phone face.

"What?"

Davecki shook his head, "The dirty bugger."

"Okay. Okay, I give. I don't want to know what you're talking about."

Davecki cut a quick glance at Stanski, grinned, said, "Looks like my phone is at the Price of War memorial."

"Seriously?"

Davecki said, "Catch!" He tossed the phone across the table.

Stanski dropped his fork with a clatter and snagged the flying phone like he was Davante Adams. "Hey!" he yelled.

Davecki laughed.

Stanski got the phone organized. He looked at the screen. "For a hermit, the guy gets around."

"No kidding," Davecki said. "Let's go."

"I'm not finished eating."

"Yes, you are," Davecki said. He grabbed the serving plate of burbot from under Stanski's outstretched fork, headed for the fridge, inserted the whole plate including uneaten burbot and mashed potatoes. He chugged his chocolate milk. He grabbed Stanski's plate, his plate, silverware and headed for the sink.

"Settle down, Dave" Stanski said. "You've survived overnight without your phone."

"I'll settle down when I get my phone back and the Hermit is in jail."

"On what charge?" Stanski asked, heading for the door.

"He stole my phone."

"He's returning your phone ... after a fashion."

"Okay then," Davecki said, following Stanski out the door. "Battery of a police officer."

"You had a physical altercation with him?" Stanski said getting in the squad.

Davecki fell into the passenger seat, "Assault with a banned substance."

"Give it up, Dave. You can't prove he spiked your stew. It's your word against his."

"I can get a blood test."

"Get real, that stuff only happens on TV."

"Jerk," Davecki said.

As the Ioniq rolled forward silent as a magic carpet, Davecki fumed. Stanski hid his amusement as best he could.

On the phone, Stanski watched from the squad as Davecki wandered around the memorial, searching. "Thanks, Wendy, some other time. I'll let you know." He watched as Davecki scratched the back of his neck, leaned against the stone pillar and lowered his head as if in prayer. A big black crow swooped down and landed on top of the rock pinnacle. "Unbelievable," Stanski said. Grinning, he said, "Hey, Siri, call Dave."

Davecki looked like any number of cervical vertebrae could have ruptured as he snapped his head upward. The crow sprang into the air. Davecki shook his weary head. He climbed the memorial rock like Moses going up the mountain and came down with his iPhone Ten Commandments.

"He's toying with us," Davecki said, falling into the squad.

"What do you mean us, partner?"

"Okay. Okay. He's toying with me. You happy now?"

Not hiding his amusement, Stanski said, "Immensely."

Davecki sighed. He prodded his phone. "Unbelievable."

"What?" Stanski asked.

"Battery just died."

The old Brule school, the new home of Brule Beer and Ice Cream, seemed to glide past to the rear as Stanski grinned and gunned the squad as best he could.

"I wanted to check location history," Davecki said.

"So what's the big deal? Charge it."

"I will, but irregardless, first thing in the morning we're going back to collar him. What did Warden Wendy say?"

"Irregardless isn't a word."

"Is too," Davecki said.

"She's in Mad Town for the wolf hunt hearings. Won't be back for two days."

"Let me guess, you're unavailable as well?"

Stanski huffed, "Tuesday. Court tomorrow morning. Should be done by noon."

"I'm heading out there first thing."

"Where's there?" Stanski asked.

"The bait station where I left the propane tank and Cheetos and cookies," Davecki said.

"You're a glutton for punishment, you know that, don't you?"

Davecki bent to his leg, pulled his pant leg up and scratched at the white bandage wrapped around his spider bite. "It's called being persistent. It's a character quality."

"Or mule headed and stubborn."

"Yevgeny Yevtushenko said the stubborn are the most wise," Davecki said.

"You've gotta be the wisest man on the planet then."

"Thanks," Davecki said as he wrangled his bitten calf around between both hands, rubbing and twisting. "Man this thing itches, hope it wasn't a Brown Recluse."

"That's ironic," Stanski said.

"What?" Davecki asked, pushing his pant leg back into place.

"Brown recluse? Get it?"

"No," Davecki said.

"Recluse, as in hermit," Stanski said.

"Duh," Davecki said. He pinched his eyes with his thumb and forefinger. He rubbed his nose. "Maybe I'm going into anaphylactic shock," he said.

"Add hypochondriac to mule headed and stubborn," Stanski said.

That evil of all evils, Silence, emerged as if from the dashboard vents.

Valiant Stanski fought the dread off asking, "So, you seriously think the Hermit was a lawyer and a priest?"

"That's what he said. What's more important is that he said he never goes to the river on the weekends, and that he never rescued Mercy Madigan at Hall."

Stanski drummed the steering wheel. "Well then. Somebody's lying."

"Yah think?"

20

The LEDs on the hospital equipment at the bedside blinked. The BP monitor said zero. Davecki pulled the white sheet up over Brekken Hawthorne's head. Tears streaming down his cheeks, he looked at the attending nurse, "If only she'd gotten vaccinated."

The nurse, swaddled in personal protective gear and looking ready for a space-walk, spoke through the layers of shielding, her voice emminated from nowhere and everywhere at the same time. "Wakey-wakey, Davy. Duty calls," she said.

"Huh?" Davecki said. He shifted in his recliner, opened his eyes to see Stanski standing next.

Chills ran up and down his arms to gather at the back of his neck to stand the hair there upright and at attention thanks to the memory of Harry Harrison, pistol in hand, looming over him in similar fashion.

"Get your carcass moving, Dave," Stanski said. "Mercy Madigan is missing."

"What time is it?" Davecki levered the recliner.

"Four-thirty."

"I'm retired."

"No, you're not. Get your boots on. I have coffee and a Grandma Joyce roll in the squad.

Davecki popped the last bit of cinnamon roll in his mouth and listened.

Sarah O'Grady explained. "She said she was going for a walk along the river and would be back in half an hour or so."

Mr. O'Grady reached for his wife's free hand as she rubbed a tear away with the other.

"What time was this?" Stanski asked.

"Around seven-thirty last night," Oliver said.

"By nine we went looking," Owen added.

"Why did you wait until midnight to call it in?" Stanski asked.

Three O'Gradys looked at three O'Gradys, each deferring to one another. Sarah shrugged her shoulders slightly. "Guess it's up to me." She looked to the breaking dawn sky beyond the river, "Mercy has a...." She studied the eastern sky. "Umm, she's had some...."

"Oh, for God's sake," Owen said. "She's a Madigan," he flicked a glance at his mother who glared back. "She has a history of flipping out."

"Oh, Owen, must you? She's been good for so long," Sarah said.

"Coming back has shook her," Oliver said.

"What's that mean?" Davecki asked.

Sarah teared up, continued, "Losing the baby along with being abandoned in Gurley...."

"It was the meth mostly," Owen said.

Sarah went from sad to mad in an instant, evidenced by the flame thrower look she directed at her son. Then her face softened and she looked at Stanski. "Losing the baby, being abandoned, and being addicted, well, when we got there she was really out of it."

"She told me she told you she miscarried," Davecki said.

"She may have some recall issues," Sarah said.

"It might have something to do with being a pathological liar," Owen said.

Sarah's shoulders sagged. She looked at the floor.

"That's enough, son," Oliver said.

Owen huffed, gave his father a silent stare in reply.

I wonder who would win that fight, Davecki wondered. "You knew she had the baby?" He looked at Sarah.

"Sort of," Sarah said.

"What's that mean?" Stanski asked.

Sarah didn't answer.

"They knew," Owen leaked out like a whistleblower.

Spaghetti lives, Davecki thought, reflecting on the incredibly tangled lives some people manage to get themselves twisted into.

"We found out one of the nuns stole the baby," Oliver said.

Mercy thought they didn't know, Davecki thought. Secrets, so nasty, he thought again.

"By the time we got wind of the troubles over there...." Sarah sighed, shook her head, studied her toes.

"By the time Sister Arenosa called, Mercy was in the psych ward in Ironhood," Oliver took up the tale.

"We didn't know she was pregnant until we got there," Sarah said. "We would have taken the baby and raised it as our own, but Sister Agatha and Father Christie had already vanished with the poor child."

Seriously? Davecki thought.

"Seriously?" Stanski asked. "Did you go to the authorities?"

Again, the O'Grady bunch went silent.

Owen sighed, said, "I get to tell the hard parts...."

It all sounds hard, Davecki thought.

"...Aunt Arenosa convinced them to keep it quiet for the convent's sake."

"Your sister was a nun at the convent?" Stanski asked.

"Well...no, actually," Oliver said. "Sandy...er, Sister Arenosa is Sarah's cousin, but we just told the kids to call her Aunty Arenosa."

Spaghetti, Davecki mused.

"God works in mysterious ways," Sarah said. "Mercy never knew how much we knew. With the child gone already and Mercy in such bad shape, we decided to focus all of our attention on getting Mercy help."

Tangled spaghetti, Davecki thought.

"The hospital in Ironhood recommended Windibago," Sarah said.

"The Myron County D.A. agreed to deferred prosecution if she went into treatment and got clean," Oliver said.

"Prosecute? What charges?" Stanski asked.

"Possession with intent to distribute," Owen said.

"She was facing ten years," Oliver said.

"She wasn't a criminal," Sarah said. "She was sick."

"The mental illness excuse," Owen said.

"Quit being so mean, Owen. You're not perfect," Sarah said.

"I'm well aware of that, Mom."

A mother and child reunion, Davecki thought.

"Six weeks of lock-down in a mental institution didn't help," Oliver said.

"They wouldn't even let us visit her for the first month," Sarah said.

"A couple dozen shock treatments worked wonders," Owen said.

"Knock it off, boy," Oliver said.

"She was a zombie when we got her home," Sarah said.

"It took a whole year for her to come out of it," Oliver said.

"The best year of my life," Owen said.

So it's not a brother-sister act, Davecki thought.

Oliver bristled.

Owen stared at his dad as if daring him to land another punishment for revealing family secrets.

Sarah said, "After the numbness started wearing off she started remembering the baby. When we told her Sr. Agatha and Father Christie took the baby, she regressed horribly."

"I wanted to send her back to the loony bin," Owen said.

The parents stared hard at the son.

Stanski deescalated the impending Oedipus brawl saying, "All things considered, this brings us to this morning. You think she may have had a psychotic break?" Stanski asked.

"I hope not," Sarah said.

"She just got lost," Oliver said.

"Knowing Mercy, probably both," Owen said.

This has been rehashed forever between them, Davecki thought. He said, "Well, we won't find her gathering background. Where was her PLS? What was she wearing?"

"PLS?" Oliver asked.

"Place Last Seen," Stanski said.

Oliver pointed across the lawn, toward the boathouse.

"She had on her red and white North Coast Cardinals windbreaker and blue jeans," Sarah said.

"Well, it's light enough now to see if we can track her."

"What do you mean *we*?" Stanski said. He looked at his phone.

"I've got court in an hour."

"I wasn't thinking of you," Davecki said. "I was thinking of someone who knows every nook and cranny in the Brule Valley."

"The Hermit?" Oliver asked.

"None other," Davecki said.

Evil Silence reigned as a strained tension infused the group like bad aroma therapy.

Oliver looked at the floor. Owen sighed. Sarah scrubbed her face with both hands.

"What?" Stanski asked.

Nobody spoke until Owen said, "Mom?"

She shook her head no.

Owen looked at Oliver.

Oliver inhaled, looked at Stanski, then Davecki, then said, "We're pretty sure that the Hermit is Mercy's son."

Big time spaghetti, Davecki thought.

"Pretty sure?" Stanksi asked.

"Like one hundred percent sure," Owen said.

"Owen!" Sarah said.

"Give it up, Mom."

"So you've known this all along?" Stanski asked.

"A few years back Pastor Lopez rotated to the diocese. He had left doing law for the Vatican," Sarah said.

"But he still wanted to minister, is what he said," Oliver added.

"Oh, for crying out loud," Owen said. "Cut to the chase will you?"

His parents stared at him, speechless.

"As usual, I get to do the dirty work," Owen said.

"Sounds familiar," Stanski said.

"What?" all three O'Gradys said.

"Don't mind my partner," Davecki said. "But please, someone cut to the chase. Time's wasting. She's out there in the woods somewhere."

Owen plunged on, "Lopez liked to talk about his childhood in the Copper Canyon where his parents were teachers. Eventually they told him he was a bastard."

"Oh, Owen," Sarah said. "Must you be so crude?"

"Okay, does *illegitimate* make it any better?" Owen lanced his mother with a slicing glance.

"I always thought he didn't look very Mexican for a Lopez," Oliver said.

Profiler, Davecki thought.

"It didn't take many after-Mass dinners to figure it out," Sarah said.

"His parents never told him?" Stanski asked.

"Only enough to send him into the priesthood," Owen said. "Steven Jobs didn't know he had a sister until he was twenty-seven."

"God works in mysterious ways," Sarah iterated again. "How he ended up in the U.P. and so close to home is a miracle."

"Imagine his surprise upon hearing Sister Arenosa's Last Rites," Owen said.

"He got the whole story, both barrels from a deathbed confession," Oliver said.

He really is a shotgun man, Davecki thought.

"Can you imagine the shock and trauma," Sarah said. "Finding out you're a...." Sarah hesitated.

"You can say bastard, mom," Owen said.

"...an orphan," Sarah said. "That you were basically stolen and brought to another country?"

"He showed up on our porch one day without his collar and announced that he was our grandson," Oliver said.

"How'd he know?" Stanski asked.

"He said Sandy...Arenosa...told him everything on her death bed," Sarah said.

"He cussed all three of us out royally and drove right back down that driveway. I was so mad at him for using that kind of foul language in front of Sarah," Oliver said.

"I had to look up Spanish cuss words after that," Owen said, smirking.

"Owen!" Sarah said.

"Take it easy, mom."

"You need to take this seriously, son," Oliver said.

"I do?"

"Yes, you do," Sarah said.

Is that smoke coming out her ears? Davecki wondered.

"Sarah, my queen, settle down. Owen's just jealous," Oliver said.

"Damn right," Owen said. "You've been enabling him too long."

Enabling who? Davecki thought. He looked at Stanski.

"You mean your dad?" Stanski asked.

"Hell no," Oliver said.

All eyes were on Sarah.

Davecki derailed the precipitous rage by saying, "You've been helping the Hermit all these years, haven't you?"

Sarah glared at her husband for a second too long then turned her death ray on her son. "He's our grandson. Your nephew. I'm ashamed of both of you."

"No wonder he's been able to survive all these years," Stanski said.

"Do you know how to reach him?" Davecki asked.

"No," Sarah said. "He would just show up whenever he needed anything, and he never asked for much."

"But he sure helped himself when we weren't here," Oliver said.

"I tried to set things out," Sarah said

Secrets and spaghetti, Davecki thought. A nasty recipe.

"I see," Stanski Anne Lamotted.

Davecki studied Stanski, maybe those Continuing Ed classes are working, he thought.

"Do you think you can find him, Mr. Dravecki?" Sarah asked.

After all we've been through? You still don't know my name? Davecki thought. He said, "All I can do is try."

21

"One-eighty-two, radio," Stanski said upon keying the mic.

"Go ahead, Stan," Dispatch Michelle said.

"Get a message to Clerk Tisher, if you would; I'm not going to make court today." He hesitated briefly, added, "please."

"As long as you've asked nicely," Michelle said. "For a minute there I was going to give you grief; Tisher's going to be very unhappy."

"Tell her she's helping save a lost soul," Stanski said.

In more ways than one, Davecki thought.

"Roger," Michelle replied.

"This is the place I left the bait yesterday," Davecki said. He picked up the empty tin plate. "Litter. Seems unhermitlike."

"How's that?" Stanski asked.

"Leaving litter. He said yesterday that picking up litter is how he got Oliver's book and hat."

"Well," Stanski said, "leaving out morsels and tidbits for a wayward grandson is a weird variation on litter, I guess.

"Equally weird is breaking and entering your grandparents' house," Davecki said.

"You've been off patrol too long, pal. Kids these days don't think twice about stealing from their parents, grandparents, and close family," Stanski said.

"Did I ever tell you about that passage about ungrateful kids written in hieroglyphics on that Egyptian rune?" Davecki asked.

"Many times," Stanski said. He pulled the tin plate from Davecki's hand, said, "For now we have bigger issues." He whacked the tin plate against his free hand. "Maybe Mercy stumbled upon this," Stanski said.

"Anything's possible, but she wouldn't take the propane," he looked at Stanski, "would she?"

"Point taken." Stanski looked around, "Man, the woods get

thicker and thicker this time of year." He tossed the tin plate to the forest floor, took out the DEET and sprayed the back of his neck, his free arm, and his legs. "Get my back, will yah?" he asked, handing the can to Davecki.

Davecki fogged Stanski's back, his own arms, legs and neck, handing the can to Stan who returned the favor, doing Davecki's back.

"Gives new meaning to, I got your back," Stanski said.

"True," Davecki said. He looked around. "Well, I know that the raccoon took off in that direction," he said. He pointed north. "But exactly where we went, I can't know. It all looks the same with all the green."

"You can't know?" Stanski asked.

"Give my grammar a break, partner," Davecki said. He picked up the tin plate and proceeded to tramp uphill in what he hoped was the right direction. Walking slow, looking for sign, he eventually said, "There's a broken twig."

"Good man," Stanski said.

They followed the spoor uphill, away from the river, and through the woods, to not Grandmother's house they went.

Half an hour of tramping around in the general direction of the Percival Mine and the Brule River escarpment, brought Stanski to the question, "Are we lost, Dave?"

"Lost is a relative term."

"How relative?"

"Like in, we aren't technically lost, after all, we are in Wisconsin and we are in the Brule State Forest, and we are uphill from the river, but I don't have a firm sense of precise location at the moment," Davecki explained.

"How comforting."

"You should try this while stoned to the high heavens on some concoction of home grown psilocybin and mollusk toxin."

"Slugs are toxic?" Stanski asked.

"They are now, at least to me," Davecki said. He cast a wider view around the green leafy world. "Wish that dang raccoon would appear. She knows where she's going," Davecki said. He pulled out his phone. "Cool, a signal." He launched the compass utility. The on-screen compass spun and spun like a pinwheel in a stiff wind. "Rats," he said. He showed the phone to Stanski.

"What the heck?"

"Must be magnetic rock around here," Davecki said. "Only thing to do is head back down toward the river, I guess. And start over."

"Or," Stanski said, "we could follow that."

Davecki looked where Stanski pointed. A fat raccoon, raised up on hind legs, was looking at them from thirty feet away.

"Eleanor?" Davecki asked.

"Chitter-chit."

"Nice to see you again, girl," Davecki said.

"You told me you can't say *girl* anymore these days," Stanski said.

"Raccoons aren't woke," Davecki said.

"Yet," Stanski said.

Eleanor lowered herself and walked away Renee.

"Here we go," Davecki said.

Two ridges, a ravine, and a plank by a spring later, Eleanor traversed a rocky incline and jumped up on a boulder. The boulder was covered side to side with lichen except in the center where the green was worn away like a rut in a road. She jumped up to another boulder as if climbing steps. She looked back at Stanski and Davecki, jumped again and reversed course up the virtual cliff face on a path nearly invisible to the naked eye.

"Here we go," Davecki iterated again as he climbed the stairway to not heaven.

Up they went, twelve steps until Davecki poked his head up over the ledge of a broad shelf of basalt the size of a semi truck and trailer.

The Hermit of the Brule looked up from the Hillerman in his hands. Seeing Davecki's head looking around like a wary gopher emerging, he put the book face down and open on an old nail keg upended next to the green and white webbed lawn chair he sat upon. One of the chair arms sported a white plastic arm rest. The other arm rest was sans plastic and bent away at an acute angle. Hermit rose and said, "This is the first time in twelve years I've ever had visitors. Kind of a shock. I'd offer tea, but it's too much of a hassle going to the tea room and bringing it back up here."

Standing on the ledge rock apron spread out from the cave mouth, Davecki handed the tin plate to Hermit and said, "Holy mackerel, what a view."

The quartet gazed out across the Brule Valley, across the green carpet of tree tops, across the undulating waves of not grain all the way to the blue diamond of Lake Superior fifteen miles distant. The wolf's head of water making up the western terminus of the St. Lawrence Seaway seemed to be tipped at an upward angle toward Minnesota and Canada beyond.

"Yes, great view. Never fails to satisfy me whenever I actually take time to fully appreciate it," Hermit said. "Sorta takes on a different meaning now, sharing it with newcomers."

Is that a good or bad new meaning, Davecki wondered.

"Impressive," Stanski said.

"Inspirational even," Davecki said.

"Chitter-chit," Eleanor said. She took a bite of a snickerdoodle. The scent of French vanilla and cinnamon added a nice touch to the astonishing view.

After a long minute of impressive, inspirational, exceptional, gazing, Hermit broke the trance asking, "To what do I owe the pleasure of your company today?"

Your mother is lost in the woods and we need your help finding her, Davecki didn't say. "We're wondering if you've had any recent contact with the lady you didn't rescue at Hall Rapids the other day," he said.

Stanski eyeballed Davecki with a *what?* look.

Hermit didn't answer. He put the tin atop the book and bent down to pick up Eleanor as she clawed her way up his pants leg. "Chica mala. You're ruining my favorite pair of pants," he said.

Your only pair, by the looks of them, Davecki thought.

Hermit swung the raccoon around in a practiced overhead twirl, landing Eleanor on his right shoulder.

Looks like the reverse of the dismount at the tea room, Davecki thought.

"You're the first people I've seen in, well," he looked back at Lake Superior, he appeared to be thinking hard, his brow furrowed, "in, well, besides your visit the other day," he nodded at Davecki, "in well, years, actually."

He's lying, Davecki thought. Too complicated an answer. *In many words is folly,* he recalled the Proverb.

Stanski said, "Cut the crap, man. You've been in regular contact with the O'Gradys. They told us everything. Your mother is missing and presumed lost in the woods on some sort of psychotic holiday. Nobody knows the valley like you. You want to help us find her? Or would you prefer being thrown in jail?"

Whoa, Davecki thought as he joined the incredulous looks from Chica Mala and Mala Hermit.

Stanski glared back, fully projecting his law enforcement aura.

More C.E. classes on the new policing for you, Davecki thought.

"Tut tut," Hermit said. "Such toxic masculine hostility is entirely without effect here," Hermit scolded.

Stanski huffed. He shrugged. "Well, it was worth a try. How about it, then? You want to help us find your mother?"

Hermit studied his visitors. He stroked his beard.

"What do you think, El?" he asked.

Eleanor scratched behind her ear. She gazed thoughtfully at the sky. "Chitter-chit."

"Yes, I know it was mean of her to throw me away like an unwanted toy."

Spare me the clichés Davecki thought.

"Chitter-chitter," Eleanor clacked her teeth.

"Yes, it helped to find out that was untrue, that mom and dad stole me from her."

"Chitter-chit-chit."

"You're right about that. You did get a second chance when your mom got hit."

"Chit-chit. Hiss," Eleanor said, adding a little purring like a cat getting a belly rub.

"If you say so girl," Hermit said. He raised his bearded face to the sky. "Fweet-fweet-fweet," he whistled.

Stanski and Davecki looked confused.

"Calling in the troops," he said as he walked to the nail keg. Displacing the tin plate with a rattle, he picked up the Hillerman. He opened the book to the very back. He stood and read.

"Warden Wendy's gonna love this," Stanski whispered.

"Yep," Davecki heeded Proverbs seventeen about fools seeming wise if they keep their mouth shut. Hermit continued reading.

A black dot appeared in the blue sky and grew until Crow skidded to a stop on the ledge. In its black beak, a white plastic propeller, broken, not stirred. Crow walked to a heap of drone parts in the corner, dropping the prop on top of the pile.

"That explains why Juhaun Boovey's drones keep going missing," Stanski said.

"Caw. Caw," Crow said.

Hermit closed the book. He walked to Davecki. "Now you can return it," he said, handing the book over. "I like Manuelito getting involved."

"Caw. Caw," Crow said.

"I know, Elvis. It is unusual. But circumstances are extraordinary today," Hermit said. He looked at the lawmen, "Nothing to it but to do it. Shall we?" he swept his arm in the direction of the exit or entrance. "Elvis? Go fly a kite. See if you can find Ms. Mercy."

The crow launched with a caw-caw, flapping black wings to the cobalt sky, the sunlight reflecting silver-like from the backs of his glossy wings.

"You're willing to help then," Davecki said.

"All we can do is try," Hermit answered.

22

Elvis flew point. Eleanor ran point. Hermit kept pace with the ringtail as it shuttled through the hardwoods, brush, swamp, and woodland meadows. The out-of-shape boys huffed and puffed in pursuit. The Black Ops Airborne, Marine Recon Racoon, and Special Forces Hermit led the law through the boonies, around swamp holes, across bogs, and up and down ravines. Every now and then Elvis circled above, cawing directions.

"Where are we headed?" Davecki asked, heaving and huffing like Thomas the Tank Engine.

"Skid May's Ledges," Hermit said.

Both hands on his knees, Davecki looked at Stanski who leaned against an ash tree for support. Both lawmen rasped breath in and out like thoroughbreds blowing after The Derby's nine furlongs.

Hermit on the one hand, and Eleanor on the other, studied the suffering softies, amusement twinkling from their devilish eyes.

"Skid May's? I've never heard of that," Davecki said between gasps. "I've always heard it as just May's Ledges."

"That's because you're a blow-in," Hermit said.

"Blow-in?" Stanski asked.

"A newcomer. Someone the wind recently blew into the valley," Hermit said.

Takes one to know one, Davecki thought.

Elvis swooped past with a "Caw-caw-caw."

"What was that?" Stanski asked.

"We head to the river and wait," Hermit said.

On the bank of the beautiful, the beautiful not Jordan, Stanski and Davecki entered their not heavenly rest, breathing returning to normal. Hermit and Eleanor played a game of fetch the stick, raccoon acting the part of dog. Crow flew back, cawing like a work whistle on the Flintstones. All eyes turned upriver to see the high bow of an old red-painted Grumman coming around the not mountain when she come.

The old canoe's nose stuck in the air like a debutante making a grand ballroom entrance.

The debutante in charge at the stern, wielding a single paddle, got the Grumman sideways in the waters gathering for the rush across the ledge rock of May's—or Skid May's—Ledges. The beat up old Grumman spun around like a Tilt-A-Whirl basket full of joy riders at the Hayfield County Fair. The ghost of old Skid May used the torrent of water to send the Grumman's bow so high in the air it looked like an exclamation point dancing along the river's compound sentence. The debutante was the dot at the bottom. The dot vanished under the frothy cascade of water. The canoe slammed down onto the rapids with a hollow boom echoing off the woods watching.

Forthwith, the rapids spit the empty vessel out like a bit of aluminum foil contaminating a baked potato bite at Friday Night Fish Fry.

"No PFD," Davecki said.

"No helmet," Stanski said.

"Chitter-chit," Eleanor chimed in.

"Caw caw-caw," Elvis called from above.

Hermit eschewed words, rushing recklessly into the rampaging river.

"HANG IN THERE, MOM!" he hollered as the waterlogged and coughing Mercy popped to the surface. Hermit crashed into the surging stream, splashing like a big black Labrador retriever. With one hand he reached out, he reached out to touch someone.

Mercy careened past in the clutches of the Brule.

Unlike God reaching out for Adam on the Sistine Chapel ceiling and missing by millimeters, two hands met in a Brule River baptism. Hermit's stability swung his mother from the cascade like a fantastic tango move, pulling Mercy into Hermit's arms in a non-COVID-approved hug of stunning proportions. The embrace lasted a few seconds until Hermit held Mercy away. His whiskers moved indicating speech drowned out by the racket of water over rock.

Mercy shook her head like she was accepting a wedding proposal.

The duo hugged again.

Davecki sing-songed, "The mother and child reunion is only a commotion away."

"You're actually funny for once," Stanski said, studying his partner.

"Well, you're going to get a big laugh out of that, then," Davecki said.

"What?" Stanski asked, turning back to the watery scene playing in the rapids.

Mercy and Hermit broke their embrace. Mercy chased the paddle. Hermit ran down the canoe as it floated in the shallows below the rapids.

"They're making a run for it!" Stanski said, dashing for the riverside trail.

Davecki ran after Stanski.

Hermit grabbed the Grumman's afterdeck and, like a furry Sasquatch, spun the canoe on its nose. Water dumped, Hermit righted the boat, steadied it as Mercy returned, paddle in hand. She stepped into the middle of the boat. Eleanor leaped to the bow seat. Hermit pushed off to deep water. He sprang like a water strider to the stern seat, took the paddle from Mercy, and dug deep into the flow, scooting the getaway canoe from the scene of the not crime.

Stanski and Davecki ran to the brush enshrouded shore. They battled through entangling limbs reaching the downriver shore in time to watch the newly blended family speed past on fast water. Hermit raised his paddle in salute. Mercy, from her Queen of Sheba seat amidships, waved a shy single handed finger-flutter at the hapless lawmen.

Looks familiar, Davecki thought.

Eleanor reared on her haunches from the bow seat. She stuck out her pink tongue, waggling it in the air like Snoopy doing a big bleah on TV. She waved both paws at the landlubbers. Hermit laughter rose above the rush of the rapids. Mercy's high pitched trill of delight sang counterpoint. The canoe's stern vanished around the bend.

Stanski looked at Davecki.

Davecki rubbed his chin. "Did that raccoon just flip us a double Fickle Finger of Fate?"

"I do believe she did, sir," Stanski answered directly and without irony, satire, or scorn for once.

"Can you beat that?" Davecki asked.

"I don't think so," Stanski said.

Just then, Elvis swooped down the river at speed, flying at the lawmen like an Alfred Hitchcock extra. At the last moment, Elvis pulled a 5G climb showing his shiny black belly. A squirt of white liquid shot out from under her tail landing with a splash at Davecki's Blackwing boot toes.

"Guess I was wrong," Stanski said as Elvis peaked out, did a Flying Wallenda somersault, cawed three times, and disappeared downriver.

"Pretty grand exit, I'd say," Davecki said.

23

"How long has it been?" Davecki asked. He grabbed the smooth maple handle of the single basket hamburger griller. He lifted it from the notch in the stick holding the caged meat over the open flame. He opened the blackened stainless steel cage holding his nutrition. He flopped the well charred forty percent venison, sixty percent beef burger onto the paper plate sitting on the stump next to the fire ring.

"Six weeks," Stanski said. Seated on his own stump across the fire ring, he smudged mayonnaise from the corner of his mouth with the hand not holding his own thick burger.

"No burglaries since?" Davecki picked up his quart jar of home squeezed apple juice and drank.

"No sign of the Hermit or any of his posse," Stanski said. He bit off almost more than he could chew, but, with effort he masticated and swallowed hard. Tears bulged from the corners of his eyes. He picked up the pint jar of apple juice sitting on the stump next. He chased the burger bite down. He backhanded the tears.

"Shed not a teardrop on the flame of fire," Davecki quoted.

"This isn't a funeral pyre," Stanski shot back.

"Nothing can raise my ire tonight, Stan. It's too lovely out," Davecki said.

"From puns I will retire," Stanski said.

"Thus avoiding another quagmire," Davecki said.

Stanski eyeballed Davecki, "Out of the goodness of my heart I'm going to let you have the last word this time."

"Mucho Gracias," Davecki said. He grinned. He asked, "Warden Wendy eradicated Hermit's hangouts?" He put a thick slice of red tomato on his burger.

"Like they never existed," Stanski said. He took another chomp out of his fat-bunned burger. The thick slice of tomato in the fold pushed out the backside of the sandwich like a lovely band of red sky at night sailor's delight. "The DNR returned fifty-five propane tanks to Cenex."

"Amazing," Davecki said. He picked up a thick white slice of Vidalia onion, laying it on top of the tomato slice on his fat bun.

"Man, this apple juice is good," Stanski said, slurping. "Owen traded his Tesla in on a Winnebago motor home."

"Seriously?" Davecki said. He spooned a gob of mayonnaise on underside of the top bun.

"He's taking his 'rents on a slow tour up the Alaska highway."

Davecki paused, putting his bun atop his masterpiece burger. "'Rents?"

"You're such a Neanderthal," Stanski said. "Ollie and Sarah."

"Oh, his parents," Davecki said. "Why can't you just talk like a normal person, Stan?"

"Normal is just a setting on a dryer," Stanski said.

"You're not funny. You know that, don't you?"

"So I've been told," Stanski said.

"That's a nice long ride up the Al-Can. It'll heal their relationship," Davecki said. He took a chomp of burger.

"Or the men will kill one another by Fort Nelson." Stanski swigged more apple juice.

"Sarah could live in peace for once then," Davecki said.

"How come I get only a pint of juice and you get a whole quart jar?" Stanski asked.

Davecki gulped burger, said, "Because you're mysteriously never around in the fall when I'm juicing."

Stanski grabbed the fire-poking stick. He stirred the coals. Bright orange sparks rose to the leaves fluttering on the hot air.

"You think they'll ever get the whole family together again?" Davecki asked. He bit more burger. The white onion slice poked out the back of the burger like a toothy smile.

"I'd say it's a hundred percent likely they'll be dining on halibut in Homer real soon," Stanski said.

"You're probably right," Davecki said.

"By the by," Stanski said. "You still owe me ten bucks."

Davecki sighed. He picked up his Thermacell thingy. "You know," he said, waving the unit toward Stanski, "there's only one thing wrong with this."

"What's that?" Stanski asked.

"It doesn't keep you from bugging me."

"You're all heart, pal." Stanski picked up a chunk of firewood. He tossed it on the flames. Sparks danced to the high heavens above.

SPONSORS

Stormy Kromer, Ironwood, MI = Gold Level

Turner Enterprises, Iron River, WI = Gold Level

Iron River Pizza Parlor = Silver Level

Zifko Gas, Ashland, WI = Platinum Level

Anonymous = Platinum Level